About the author

Ian McFall

McFall Emigrated from the UK in 1967 with his wife and twin children. He became a US citizen in 1974. He worked for Boeing on several 737 and SST projects as well as classified projects involving helicopter warfare. He moved to California in 1970 just as the lights were going out in Seattle and spent 10 years in the Semiconductor industry before becoming president of a division of the Eaton Corporation in Sunnyvale California.

McFall started his own small software business, which he sold before retiring to the Pacific Northwest in 2007. After an unsuccessful attempt to run as County Commissioner, he ran the Economic Development department for Jefferson County. He was an active volunteer with the US Coast Auxiliary and was elected commander of the 60-member Port Ludlow Flotilla. He and his wife Glenys moved to Silverdale when she was diagnosed with terminal cancer.

Since his wife passed away, McFall has built a 4-seat kit plane for his nephew, who lives in South Africa. He obtained a US airworthiness certificate for the plane, flying it in the USA for 40 hours before removing the wings and shipping it in a container to South Africa, where he obtained a South African airworthiness certificate for the plane. It was harder to get the South African Airworthiness certificate than it was to build the plane. He has also restored a 1969 Cherokee to airworthy condition.

McFall started flying gliders as a cadet in the Air Training Corps in the UK while still in high school. He now has over 2000 hours in gliders, has flown several flights over 500 miles without an engine, and reached altitudes higher than typical airline routes. Captain McFall now teaches 14-18-year-olds to fly with the Civil Air Patrol in Washington. Until recently he managed the glider program for Washington State CAP. In the last two years, he has given over 200 glider rides to CAP cadets and won the "Instructor of the Year" award for the Pacific NW in 2015. He is now the National Glider Program Manager, coordinating the activities of 46 Gliders, 22 Tow Planes, and 150 volunteer pilots.

He has written many articles about flying, boating and other life experiences for 20 years. He writes a monthly column for "Soaring Magazine" a nationally distributed magazine of the Soaring Society of America. This is his first full-length novel.

Other books by Ian McFall

Cats, planes and terrorists: A compendium of short stories and articles written between 1980 and 2015

The Last Crusade. (Book 1) A romantic thriller about Israel's fight against a United Islamic foe.

The Last Crusade. (Book 2) (December 2020) A fictional revelation about the lifestyle of the young Mohamed causes millions to abandon the faith.

From Melting Pot to Cesspool in 60 years. (May 2021) An immigrant's account of Social Entropy in the USA.

Copyright.

Credits

Editors Marilyn Knutson, Chris Graham, and Annie Colcothar
Proofreaders. Tammy Lehman, Karen Burgan
Military Aviation advisors. General Robert Hall USAF (ret).
Colonel R. Duncan Brown
USMC (Ret.)
Cover design. Winifred Wilson

Preface

During Donald Trump's controversial first term he implemented several changes in US foreign policies that had far-reaching effects on World Affairs. Trump moved the US Embassy to Jerusalem and cut funding to the United Nations, which was paying Turkish troops to oppose US forces in Syria at that time. This move prompted ISIS, which was funded primarily by Iran, to seek the support and cooperation of other Arab states in the Middle East.

Trump also cut aid to the Palestinians and provided Missile Defense Systems to Israel, the only real Democratic state in the Middle East and the USA's only ally there. Trump's domestic policies opened up the Arctic oil to exploration. He also prevented the oil pipeline from Russia to Germany from becoming a reality. This was easily accomplished by threatening to end US defense agreements with Germany if the pipeline was approved.

The opening of the Alaska oil fields and more favorable policies regarding fracking quickly made the USA independent of Arabian oil supplies. The US found itself in a position to supply surplus oil to China at well below Middle Eastern prices. China's voracious appetite for energy also forced them to buy coal from the USA too, fulfilling a long-standing promise of the Trump regime to bring miners' jobs back to the USA.

Falling oil prices and the shortage of US currency used to pay for the oil, pressured the Arab Countries to act. They buried many of their tribal hatchets to form local coalitions. Soon, both Sunni and Shia Muslim countries embraced ISIS as a means to retaliate against "US tyranny". Within two years, the "United Islamic Alliance" (UIA) was formed with funding from all of the Muslim

Arab States. Within the Arab sphere of influence, only Turkey stood on the fence.

The threat to Israel was intense. The UIA now had access to sophisticated weapons supplied by the US to Saudi Arabia and began buying fighters from Russia, equipped with the latest Electronic Warfare technology.

US Domestic policy during World War II, a chance encounter by a widowed Brit named Andrew Hollingsworth and an attractive French journalist, led to a surprising end to what had been expected to be a short, one-sided Arab/Israeli conflict.

Manzanar 1942

Koji Imakita's attention wandered again to the window of the Quonset hut. The wind whined through the gaps around the window frame, and somewhere, a loose screen door slammed incessantly back-and-forth. Outside, the tumbleweed had formed a long line, its progress across the endless gray sagebrush halted by the barbed-wire fence surrounding the camp. Beyond the fence, standing like black cardboard cutouts on an indigo horizon, the descending gloom of the desert terminated in the stark outline of the Sierra Nevada.

The Japanese internment camp was scratched out of the sagebrush at Manzanar, in the Owens Valley, 16 miles northeast of Bishop California. Most of the interns had been there since the camp had opened one year ago. Japanese families from all over California had being herded together in local transit centers and were then moved to the camp by military bus. Early arrivals were put up the big army tents, which were the only shelter until the Quonset huts arrived.

Every able-bodied man and all the boys over 16 years of age had worked for three months to erect the huts, dig wells and lay water and sewer pipes. It was not unusual for temperatures in Manzanar to hit 100° by noon, and every single laborer had suffered the ill-effects of dehydration and sunstroke. Even the guards who supervised the work from makeshift shade had suffered from the intense summer heat.

In the summer, the huts turned out to be useless. The corrugated metal from which they were made became so hot that, within two hours of sunrise, the huts were like ovens. Many of the families returned to the tents until the fall, when the winds started and it began to cool off. The cool of the winter was welcome and Koji liked to watch the violent Sierra storms lash the mountains in the distance. The mountaintops seemed to absorb the violent blue of the lightning then, a half-minute later, the thunder would rumble across the valley. His mother was terrified of the thunder, and it pleased Koji that he was not afraid and he would hold her close to him until it passed. Although the thunder frightened her to the point where she would tremble, she enjoyed uninhibited comfort in the strength of her only son.

Koji missed his mother. She had fallen ill and had been admitted to the camp hospital three weeks ago. He had been allowed to visit her only twice and each time she seemed paler and weaker. Today was December 20, 1942, Koji's 17th birthday and he felt desperately sad that he would not see his mother on this day.

The sound of his father's voice quickly redirected Koji's attention back to the calligraphic Japanese characters he had been brushing onto a whitewashed board.

"Hurry so that you may finish your work while there is still enough light", his father addressed him curtly in Japanese. Koji obediently went back to his work.

"You will never learn to write in Japanese if your mind is elsewhere." The voice behind him was softer now and Koji knew that his father had seen his work, and was pleased that he had chosen to take the classes organized by the interns and was making some progress. Until they were interned, his father had loved America but did not want his son to forget the finer elements of his Japanese heritage.

At that moment, the door of the hut burst open and a uniformed Guard entered, a rifle slung over his shoulder. The wind swirled the blown sand around his outsized army boots.

"Which one of you assholes is Imakita?" yelled the young guard, scanning the faces in the hut, now silent except for the wind howling through the open door and screeching out through the narrow gaps in the window frames. The half dozen small children in the hut clung, wide-eyed, to their mothers. It was unusual for the guards to enter the huts, more in deference to the serene nature of the inmates, which was respected by most of the guards, rather than to any camp rules.

The guard stood in the doorway, holding the door against the wind, waiting for a response.

"Imakita," he said again pronouncing the 'I' as 'eye' instead of 'ee' as in keep.'

"Father, I think he means you," Koji said quietly to his father in Japanse. Koshi ushered his father forward, defiantly returning the young soldier's malevolent stare. He waited deliberately until the soldier shifted his eyes to his father.

"This is my father, Imakita-san; he doesn't understand much English" Koji had carefully emphasized the 'san' and the implied message that his father should be treated with respect, was not lost on the soldier.

"San, bullshit!" the soldier exclaimed, "You assholes are prisoners of war and you don't get no 'san' bullshit around here. Now get you asses outside right now."

Koji, infuriated by the disrespect from the young soldier, exploded.

"I'm an American Citizen! I was born here just like you!" Koji had stepped forward, his face thrust defiantly close to that of the young soldier, who was no more than three or four years older than himself. The guard stepped back, unslinging his rifle in one sweeping motion. In unison, like a well-choreographed ballet, the mothers each clutched their children, turning each little face away from the scene, covering each small ear with a protective hand, expecting the shot to be fired.

The guard leveled the rifle at Koji's chest.

"Get your fuckin' ass outside right now Mister Fuckin' American Citizen and take this old asshole with you" hissed the young soldier, motioning toward Koji's father with his rifle. The elder Imakita bowed very slightly and went to the door, struggling to hold it open against the wind. Koji followed him; his eyes boring into the soldier in unconcealed rage. The soldier took the rifle in his left hand, vaguely threatening those remaining in the hut, and backed clumsily out through the door, letting it slam closed in a violent gust of wind.

The soldier motioned Imakita toward the Camp Administration quarters in the corner of the compound. Koji had begun to explain the disrespectful exchange to his father but was quickly interrupted.

"Shut up and get moving" urged the soldier. He held the peak of his fatigue cap and turned his head to shelter his face from the wind, his rifle slung casually in the crook of his right arm. Koji walked proudly beside his father, whom he dwarfed, his head held high despite the wind and blowing sand. He tried to visualize his attack on the soldier cowering against the wind.

"Don't get any ideas asshole!" the soldier seemed to have read his mind and Koji, thinking that the rifle might now be pointed at the center of his back, kept walking in the direction of the Administration building. He tried his best to shelter his father from the wind and blowing sand.

The administration building was oppressively hot, a big cast-iron stove crackled behind the fat sergeant's desk.

"You can get back to the guardroom Corporal." the sergeant was politely firm. He looked up at the older man and pronouncing his name correctly asked.

"Mister Imakita?"

"This your son?" the sergeant addressed the elder man. Imakita looked to the son for a translation.

"This is my father, Imakita-San, He doesn't understand much English"

"OK, then you better go in and talk to the camp commander with your father. Go through that door there." The sergeant's voice was gentle but he quickly averted his eyes from Koji's inquisitive look.

"Through that door," the sergeant said again pointing a stubby finger at the door on the other side of the room. Koji ushered his father through the door without offering an explanation. The camp commander rose from behind the wooden desk.

"Please sit down Imakita-San, are you... " He hesitated while he found Koji's name from the file on his desk, then asked, "are you Koji?"

"Yes, my father doesn't understand English very well so the soldier outside told me to come in with my father." Koji looked willfully at the camp commander, anger from the confrontation with the corporal still burning in his eyes.

"I'm afraid I have some very bad news for you both," the commander announced quietly after the two had sat down. Koji thought his heart had stopped. The bad news could only be about his mother.

"Is she worse?" Koji asked. He could barely speak and his father, immediately sensing his son's distress, pleaded with his eyes for an explanation.

"I'm afraid she's dead son, she died at 4:15 this afternoon. We did all we could." The Commander put his arm around the boy's shoulder and patted him gently. Koji shrugged him off.

"Tell me my son Koji, is it your mother? Is she dead?" his father asked in Japanese. Koji could not answer, the tears already streaming from his eyes. He nodded to his father, unable to look at him directly.

"I'll leave you two alone for a moment or two," the commander said. For the very first time in his life, Koji embraced his father. They stood, wordless, with their arms around each other. Koji's father buried his face in his son's shoulder and began to sob. It seemed to Koji that his father had suddenly become very small and very frail. The Camp Commander returned shortly with the doctor, who was still wearing a white hospital coat, a stethoscope around his neck. Father and son parted quickly, embarrassed by their public display of emotion.

"This is Dr. McDonald; he attended your mother Koji." Koji wiped the tears from his cheeks with the heel of his hand. Koji's father stared vacantly out of the window, oblivious to the entrance of the doctor. The doctor spoke directly to Koji.

"Your mother has been sick for some time, I'm afraid. The journey here and the heat of the summer aggravated her condition. If she had been diagnosed earlier, we might have been able to save her."

Koji's mind was numb. The doctor rambled on, using medical terminology which, for Koji, might as well have been another language.

"Would you like to see her now?" The doctor finally sensed that neither Koji nor his father understood what he was saying. Koji formed the question in Japanese for his father but when he spoke, his voice cracked with emotion and he had to begin again.

"I would like to see her alone first Koji." his father said in Japanese. Koji repeated his father's request to the commander in English.

"I understand; tell your father to follow the doctor, you can wait here." Koji motioned for his father to follow the doctor and then sat down. He suddenly felt very tired.

Several days later, Koji sat outside the hut with his father. No one spoke. Both gazed out at the mountains where clouds were gathering quickly, casting deep shadows over the mountainsides. Koji sat with his back against the curved metal wall of the hut, his knees drawn up tightly to his chest.

"She wouldn't have died if they hadn't made us come here. The doctor said that." Koji spoke softly in Japanese as though talking to himself.

"Why did they bring us here father? I don't understand! We belong in this country as much as they do. I was born here and before they bombed Pearl Harbor, Frankie Quinlan and I were talking about joining the Airforce so we could fight the Japanese and the Germans." Koji looked at his father, who shrugged.

"My old country has behaved without honor Koji. I am ashamed of what happened at Pearl Harbor." He paused slightly, "I have been dishonored by my own people."

"I am glad we bombed them!" replied Koji, "these people are barbarians. That soldier called you an asshole. They have no respect, even for their own kind. They are pigs!" Imakita-san turned to look at his son.

"That young man is only three or four years older than you, Koji. His father was killed and his elder brother was maimed at Pearl Harbor. He has good reason to hate the Japanese"

"But I am not Japanese. I was born here just as he was and look at what they have done to us. They have taken everything, our home, our livelihood, and they keep us penned up like animals in this stinking desert. They wouldn't even let us bury my poor mother in the true Shinto way." Koji spoke with venom in coarse Japanese, and he had to use his stomach muscles to get the harsh words out.

"I hate them! I wish I could return to Japan and join the Imperial Nippon Airforce so that I too could bomb them!"

"You can never return to Japan, Koji. If the Americans win the war the Japanese will be dishonored forever. If the Japanese should win, God forbid that, you would be disowned by them as a traitor because your father chose to come to America when he was not much older than you are now. You would be like the Eta in Japan. You would be one of the 'untouchables', hated by your Japanese rulers and shunned by your American neighbors."

The two fell into silence again and soon the thunder started. Koji got up and went inside the hut. He didn't want to brave the thunder without being able to comfort his mother. As left, he muttered to himself.

"Someday I will go back to Japan with honor"

Iris

Iris Hollingsworth weaved her way through the crowd that was attending her sister Fiona's second wedding reception. The newly-married couple had already left and the band had stopped playing. She wore her favorite off-white fitted dress and a French Blue Bolero jacket with long sleeves. Her wide-brimmed hat matched the dress, with a hatband that matched her jacket. She had on her trademark red pumps with three-inch heels. She looked stunning and she knew it.

Several people touched her arm as she slipped past them.

"Bye Iris, see you soon. Sorry, we didn't get to chat."

"See you next time," one of her sister's friends said, with a little cattiness in her voice.

She responded to the farewells with the easy grace of a confident woman.

"Come on Andrew, we had better go," she said as she found her husband who was in the midst of a serious conversation with a coy little brunette who either didn't know Andrew was married or didn't care.

"I don't want you to miss your plane" Iris interrupted gently, taking his arm. They walked arm-in-arm to their car.

"Who was Little Miss Goo-Goo eyes then?" asked Iris looking up into his eyes and gripping his arm tightly. She was never insecure about their relationship. Andrew was a natural flirt and attracted women like hummingbirds around a feeder. That's what had attracted her to him in the first place. He flirted with her and made her laugh.

Iris got into the driver's side of the car and Andrew closed the door for her. That was another thing she liked about her husband: he had impeccable manners. After four years of marriage, she still liked him just the way he was.

They first met at an airport. Iris' father had been in the RAF and started flying gliders competitively after he retired. Andrew was only 18 and was already a glider instructor at the club where her father kept his sailplane. He had flirted with her then and told her that he was going to win the UK Junior Gliding Championships that day.

"I am going to win it just for you Iris. You watch," he had whispered in her ear. And he did! Five years later, after he graduated from Cambridge, they were married.

"We've got plenty of time," said Andrew. "Take the A25, it's a much prettier ride than the M23"

"Ok" Iris acquiesced easily, taking off her hat and dropping it behind her seat. "I like that drive and the motorway will be awful at this time of day. I'm going to put the top down."

They got out of the car to put the soft top down. Andrew leaned over the back of the car and kissed her.

"I'm going to miss you," he said quietly

"Don't be silly" replied Iris, "You're only going to be gone four days!"

"I'll still miss you!"

They got back in the car and drove to Gatwick along the country roads that they both loved. She stopped the car at the baggage check-in and they both got out.

"Got everything darling?" she asked getting his carry-on bag from the trunk of the car.

"I think so."

When she wasn't wearing her high-heels she had to stand on her tiptoes to kiss him. She held him to her very close, feeling the warmth of his body through her flimsy dress. He kissed her with all the tenderness he had the first time. His kiss still made her weak at the knees.

"Go get 'em Tiger," she said, letting him go. She watched him enter the building and got back in the car.

Hollingsworth dozed off shortly after the plane took off. He woke up feeling strangely cold. A shiver ran through him momentarily, making him shudder. He put it down to the air-conditioning and reached up to adjust the vent. It was already closed.

Two hours later, Hollingsworth arrived in Bordeaux. He called Iris' cellphone but could reach only her voice mail. He caught a cab to the hotel near the Dassault Research Establishment in Merignac. There was a message for him at the front desk to call home urgently.

Hollingsworth pushed the speed dial on his cellphone. When his sister-in-law Fiona answered the phone, Hollingsworth shuddered again.

"It's Andrew," he said and Fiona began to cry.

"What's wrong?"

"There's been an accident, a car accident."

"Is Iris ok?" He knew she wasn't.

"Andrew..." Fiona's voice trailed off.

"Oh God!" said Andrew, holding back a primordial scream.

"She died at the scene, Andrew. It was a head-on collision. No survivors." Fiona began to cry again. There was a long stunned-silence on the telephone.

"I am so sorry Andrew. I am so sorry" Fiona blurted the words into the mobile phone.

"I'll get the next plane home Fee. Can you pick me up?" Andrew called his sister-in-law by the nick-name his wife had always used.

"Of course." she began to cry again.

Hollingsworth hung up and sat down in one of the armchairs in the hotel lobby. A young woman in an Air France flight-attendant uniform came up to him. She had heard him talking on his mobile and spoke to him in English with an almost indiscernible French accent.

"Are you ok sir?" she asked politely. Hollingsworth was ashen.

"No," he said trying desperately to hold back the tears that now flooded his eyes.

"No, I am not." he croaked the words out. "I just heard that my wife has been killed in a car accident."

The woman sat down next to him and gently took his hand. They sat in silence for several minutes.

"Stay here." The woman said softly. "I'll be right back."

When she got back, Hollingsworth had recovered his composure a little. She had a paper cup of hot tea in one hand and a miniature bottle of brandy in the other. She sat down beside him again and unscrewed the cap off the tiny brandy bottle. He smiled at her.

"In the tea please" his voice cracking with emotion.

"I've got to get back to England," Hollingsworth said quietly.

"Let me take care of that for you, give me your return ticket and I'll get you on a flight back." He fumbled in his briefcase and found his tickets.

"Thanks," he said looking up at her.

"This might take a while," she said then "rester tranquille" reverting to her native French

"D'accord" he responded automatically in French. She smiled back at him and left. He went to the front desk and canceled his reservation without much explanation. Then he called his contact at Dassault. He was glad that Jean-Claude's phone went to voice-
mail.

"Jean-Claude, Andrew here, Andrew Hollingsworth. I am at the hotel in Merignac but I just received a message about a family emergency. I have to return to Guilford immediately. I will call you when I get back to the office. I know it's important that we discuss the product feature changes you want but it will have to wait. So sorry... a bientot" he signed off abruptly.

He thought for a minute about the message he had left and thought that maybe he should call Jean-Claude again and try to speak to him personally and tell him what had happened. He decided he couldn't bear to do that. Not yet. He went back to where he had been sitting, but someone had taken his seat.

"Damn," he said to himself and found another seat nearby.

The young flight attendant returned holding Air France tickets. She was looking for him in his original seat. He got up to meet her.

"The BA flight at noon is full so I got you a flight on Air France. I explained the situation to my supervisor and he has put you on the next Air France flight out. First Class, our compliments Mr. Hollingsworth. I ordered an Uber car for you. Go to the Air France First-class ticket counter to pick up your tickets" she was beaming at him now. "You had better hurry Uber won't wait!"

"I can't thank you enough," said Hollingsworth and turned to leave. Then turning back, he said.

"I don't even know your name."

"Dominique," she said "Allez, Allez!"

Hollingsworth made it to the plane and arrived in London in a complete daze. Fiona was waiting for him at the exit gate with Iris' friend Maggie. For a few seconds, he wondered why on earth they were there, and then he remembered, and the feeling of utter devastation returned. Fiona rushed to embrace him, her tears flowing again.

"God, Andrew! I can't believe this is happening." Maggie took his carry-on bag, which he didn't realize he was holding, and then took his hand. "Let's get you home," she said.

Iris was cremated and a "celebration of her life" was held at an upscale golf club in Guilford. All the ladies wore hats, a touch that Iris would have enjoyed. As Hollingsworth mingled with the guests, several of the unattached younger ladies made it subtlety obvious to him that there was no need for him ever to be lonely. He graciously acknowledged their advances and moved on.

Hollingsworth buried his grief in his work. He arrived early and worked late, often eating out on the way home. It was three months before Hollingsworth "rejoined the land of the living," as he put it. The company benefitted a great deal from Hollingsworth's dedication and won a huge bid to re-equip the German Airforce with an upgraded product that Hollingsworth had managed to get to market months ahead of schedule. They promoted him to Product Manager and gave him a fat bonus.

At about the same time, Hollingsworth received a substantial check from the insurance company. The Hollingsworth's had taken out survivor life insurance when they got married and Iris had, fortunately, kept up the premium payments. Andrew had forgotten that they ever had insurance, except for the car.

For several weeks he would sit in his untidy study at home in the evening, wondering what he would do with the check for two hundred and fifty thousand Pounds Sterling, which remained uncashed. It wasn't until the insurance company telephoned to ask why the check had not been cashed that he took it to the bank. When he looked at his balance, he realized that he hadn't touched the ten thousand Pound bonus that was deposited directly to his account and that he had saved another three thousand eating at Wimpy's instead of the more upscale Italian places that Iris had preferred.

"I'm loaded!" he said to himself. "I'm going to quit my job and take a year off. I'm going to win the World Gliding Championship." The fact that he didn't own a glider and hadn't flown one since he was twenty years old didn't deter him. He remembered the day he had told Iris he would win the UK Junior Championships and he had. He had to hold back tears that threatened to fall into his third gin and tonic.

The World Soaring Championships are held every two years at various sites around the world. The next one was scheduled in July at Chateauroux in France.

Hollingsworth quit his job and bought a used carbon-fiber glider for £150,000. He flew nearly every day during the summer in the French Alps and went to Omarama in Australia for a month. At Christmas he went to Tempe, South Africa, for three months during the bitterly cold British Winter. He flew with some of the best pilots in the world - in the mountains, in the desert, and over the African plains. After 10 days of grueling competition, Hollingsworth finished a close second to a pilot who had won the championship twice before. He had the silver cup he was awarded engraved with words "For Iris" and went back to Britain to find a new job.

Guilford

Hollingsworth looked up from his untidy desk as his colleague Peter McFarlane walked into his office. His office was one of a row, with fake mahogany doors and a narrow window that looked out on the corridor. A plastic nameplate in a brass slide said "A. Hollingsworth". Nobody had permanent nameplates on their doors simply because nobody who worked at British Aerospace Electronics (BAE) had a permanent job.

Hollingsworth had been working there for nearly two years after returning from Chateauroux. Peter had just joined the company.

"Fancy a pint?" asked Peter. He had on his heavy overcoat and carried a wool Kangol cap in one hand, a beaten-up banker's briefcase in the other.

"Are you buying?" responded Hollingsworth, getting up from his desk. Peter, putting his cap under one arm, handed Andrew his coat that was hanging on a brass hook on the inside of the door. Peter didn't answer. Hollingsworth closed the filing cabinet drawer and locked it. He locked the office door as they left.

"Nothing classified among that crap on your desk?" asked Peter. "One of these days you're going to get nailed for your sloppy attitude toward security. You know that, don't you?" Peter raised his eyebrows

"There's nothing I'm working on that you couldn't find on the internet two years ago. So I don't see much point in all the damn security" Hollingsworth tossed his coat over his shoulder.

"Let's go!" They walked through the labyrinth of similar corridors until they came to the building lobby. Peter handed the armed guard his briefcase. It contained the latest "MotorSport" magazine and an uneaten sandwich.

"Thank you, sir, have a nice evening." The guard turned to Hollingsworth, and pressed the button to unlatch the automatic exit door. The two men left the building, and Hollingsworth decided to put on his coat.

"Where are you parked Andrew?" asked Peter

"In the South end, I was a bit late this morning." Andrew chuckled. It had been nearly eleven o'clock when he had seen Andrew arrive that morning.

"Let's take my car. I'll drop you back here. There's never any bloody parking at the Britannia."

"OK." Andrew agreed quickly. "In that case, let's eat there unless you have other plans. Dianne is still out of town, right?" Peter's wife Dianne was an international airline flight Attendant, and Peter usually ate out when she was away. The sandwich in his briefcase was several days old.

They arrived at the Britannia pub located on the banks of the River Wye in Sussex. It's a lovely old building, with a large garden in the back. The back yard has several picnic benches located in the shade of three massive oak trees. Many of the patrons take their dogs with them, and the pub provides a bowl of water and a soft blanket for the dogs to lie on. It's a popular place.

They chose a table inside, near the walk-in fireplace. It was a little too cool to sit outside. Both men remove their coats and dumped them untidily on one of the spare chairs at the table. A pretty young waitress soon appeared.

"I'll have the cod and chips please, and a pint of bitter." Andrew made eye contact with the waitress. It was three years since Iris had passed away and Hollingsworth was beginning to feel the need for some female company.

"I'll have the same, but make mine a Guinness please," said Peter

The waitress returned Andrew's pleasant smile.

"Two cod and chips, a pint of bitter and a Guinness coming right up." Andrew watched the waitress's derriere as she moved away.

"She's too young for you Andrew," said Peter smirking. Andrew hadn't shown a lot of interest in the opposite sex since Iris had died.

"But I am glad to see that you are taking an interest!" Peter laughed lightheartedly.

Andrew diverted his eyes from the pretty young thing and said in a slightly guilty tone,

"Iris' would have been forty today. I am going up to the cemetery later to leave some flowers. Would you mind making a small detour on the way back?"

"No problem." Replied Peter. "You have no idea what it's like to lose someone you have been with for nearly twenty years, Peter." Peter waited, sensing that Andrew had more to say. They had only recently become friends, and intimate conversations like this were uncomfortable.

"The worst part is coming home to an empty home. Missing her voice, her happy smile..." Andrews's voice trailed off. And Peter sensed that Andrew was about to choke up.

"No problem," said Peter again light-heartedly. He had never met Iris. He was glad that the waitress appeared with their food.

"Ah, here comes the chow!" Peter declared, anxious to change the subject.

"How did you get into the Defense Electronics game?" asked Peter, taking a piece of fish from his plate.

"I've always been into airplanes," replied Andrew. "When I was in school, all I ever wanted to do was be a test-pilot. My dad was a Harrier pilot during the Falklands War. He was shot down by "friendly fire", an oxymoron if ever I heard of one. The RAF listed the incident as a landing accident but it was established nearly ten years later that it was friendly fire. It was a terrible mistake, made by a very inexperienced young weapons officer."

"God! That's awful Andrew. So, is that what prompted you to get into Defense Electronics, your father getting killed like that?"

"No, I was only two years old at the time. I had no idea what RADAR or Electronic Warfare was all about until I got out of college and started my first job. I just wanted to get into the RAF and fly fighters."

"But you never flew in the RAF, right?"

"No, never. I joined the ATC (Air Training Corps) at 14 and flew gliders until I graduated from high school. I passed all the exams to get into the RAF College at Cranwell but when I went down there to take the medical examination, I failed. My eyesight wasn't good enough. I was devastated!"

"So, what did you do when you got out of High School?"

"I had my Glider Pilot's license through the ATC. So, I joined a gliding club and got my instructor rating and started teaching as soon as I turned 18. I was a pretty good glider pilot. I won the British Junior Gliding Championships that year. I was indestructible!" Andrew laughed and beat his chest like a gorilla.

"No kidding" Peter was impressed.

"Yeah! I'll never forget that day. It was a typical summer day. A gentle breeze and big cumulus clouds hung in the air everywhere, like giant white cauliflowers. There was lift everywhere. I already knew I was going to win the contest before the flight ended. It was my first National level race. I had finished third the day before and was now in third place overall. The leader was only a mile ahead of me very low and struggling to get home. I had enough altitude to get home at over 100 knots. I pushed the nose down and let the speed build up to 135 knots. Even at that speed, I had the airport in range. I pushed the nose down a little more and crossed the finish line at 150 knots, about 50 feet above the ground and one-tenth of a mile in front of the leader. I dumped all my water ballast as I went through the finish gate. It was spectacular! "I heard the Finish-Gate call "Good Finish, Two Seven Romeo!" over the radio. I had started in the middle of the pack and finished first so I knew I had won the day. It turned out that I was the youngest UK National Champion ever. It was amazing!

"That was also the day I first met Iris. She was the daughter of one of the contest pilots. I was smitten with her the first time I saw her but we both went off to different colleges and our paths didn't cross again until after I graduated."

"Quite a story to tell the grandkids!" said Peter

"Unfortunately, Iris and I never had any kids, but I do tell the story to my nephews!" Andrew replied, spearing another soggy chip with his fork, "You still didn't explain how you got into the EW business" Peter interjected, taking a sip of his Guinness.

"Oh yes, that was serendipity, plain and simple. After I won the Championships, quite a few people asked me to give lessons on cross-country flying. One of them was a French guy that was the founder of SGC, a Canadian company involved in Electronic Warfare Systems. I got to know him pretty well and he liked me. He got me a job as an intern at their company in England and encouraged me to take a degree in Electronic Engineering."

"You were lucky," said Peter

"Yeah! I was. I went to work for SGC after I graduated from college. They offered me a great job because they knew I was familiar with their products and how they worked. I started working in their test department and got to compare the performance of their product with others on the market"

"How did your redesign proposal go last month?" asked Peter. He was referring to a proposal that Andrew had told Peter about over lunch several weeks before. In it, Andrew had described how the current product was fading in the marketplace because it wasn't as good as several new products being offered by the Americans and the Germans. The BAE system was too slow and less effective against the most recent weaponry in the field today. The Americans were eating their lunch as Andrew put it.

"Not too good" replied Andrew. "Basically, the board rejected it. Lord Plowden needs to go. He can't even use Electronic Mail, let alone understand Electronic Warfare. It's time the old fart was put down!" Plowden was chairman of the board of directors and was rumored to be over 90 years of age.

"The old bugger slept through most of the meeting," Andrew said in a disgusted tone, waving his fork as if His Lordship himself was seated at the table. A long discussion ensued about the many "Peers of the Realm" who were put out to pasture as heads of various industries that were nationalized by the British Government after World War II. Most of those industries had failed miserably in the global markets that emerged after the war. "We should have guillotined the whole bloody lot of 'em!" declared Peter, rising to leave, and with a certain air of finality said "Let's go to the cemetery."

They drove in Peter's car, a nice Volvo with leather interior. "How long has it been now?" Peter asked gently.

"Just over three years. Sometimes it feels like yesterday."

They turned into the cemetery gateway. Andrew directed Peter to his wife's gravesite.

"Her ashes are here. She wanted to be cremated. She loved to garden."

Peter looked down at the memorial stone set in the ground engraved with the words "In loving memory…". He hadn't finished reading the memorial when he realized that the entire grave area was covered with lush clover, and tiny pansies struggled toward the sunshine from around the stone slab. None of the other gravesites nearby had either the lush cover of clover or the pansies peeking from the rock-hard ground.

"Iris loved her garden," said Hollingsworth. "I think she still does."

They both started to laugh. They drove back to the campus in a more light-hearted mood and Peter drew up to Andrews's car. As he got out, Andrew asked, "Are you going to the Paris Air Show this year Peter?" The company normally had a huge booth and twenty or thirty BAE employees were usually in attendance.

"Nah! I'm not going this year. Dianne and I are going to Ibiza for a week. Her mom is having the kids"

"Ooh la la" replied Andrew, unlocking his car, "sounds wicked! I'll see you later."

Paris

The Gulfstream 555 touched down at Le Bourget at precisely 17:00 hours, right on schedule. Hollingsworth and three other BAE employees all moved over to the left side of the plane as it taxied the kilometer and a half back to the Corporate Terminal. They craned their necks to catch a glimpse of the latest aircraft from around the world that had begun arriving for the greatest airshow on Earth.

"The 797 is here already" exclaimed one of the passengers like an excited teenager.

"Wow," said another. "Look at the size of the engines on that sucker. They are monstrous!"

The G555 came to stop some distance from the terminal. A long line of private and corporate jets awaited ground service. The airport was at its busiest handling hundreds of corporate aircraft, commuter airlines and, of course, the many prototype and demonstration aircraft that would be part of the show which would commence in two days' time. The passengers began jostling to retrieve their carry-on baggage in the small aircraft configured to carry nine passengers in comfort but not luxury. The co-pilot emerged from the cockpit, looking intense.

"Gentlemen, please take your seats. Take your seats please!" He repeated a little louder, finally getting the attention of all four passengers. "We are not ready to deplane yet. There are three aircraft ahead of us and we will be moving up the queue as they are serviced, so please remain seated until then. We will be starting and stopping for at least another 45 minutes, so please sit down."

The four men began taking their seats at each of the four windows from which they could see the exhibited aircraft. The co-pilot retreated to the cockpit, leaving the door open so that he could observe the passengers. Hollingsworth took out his iPad and began going over his notes on the presentation he was scheduled to give at the symposium which ran concurrently with the airshow. A lot of existing customers and some key potential customers wanted to know the future of BAE's IFF product line.

Hollingsworth was preparing to talk about the evolution of the product line and what would differentiate the new product they were about to release. He knew that his audience would be looking for revolution not evolution, and he didn't have much to say about that.

They finally got ready to disembark. The onboard stairway was deployed and the four men moved up to the doorway. They boarded a small van that was to take them to the customs and immigration area. Since BREXIT implementation had begun, British citizens were no longer free to enter Europe without going through customs and Immigration. It was an inconvenience, but the UK's booming exports to the USA and the old commonwealth countries more than made up for that. The Asians, Yanks, and Aussies had done business with the Brits for three-hundred years. They preferred the rogues they knew, rather than the Germans. with whom they had recently fought in bloody wars, and the French who exported only wine, cheese and perfume anyway.

The van picked up a few more people who had just disembarked from a Falcon 50 and stopped at the terminal security gate.

"Non-Eu citizens disembark here please" announced the driver in a thick French accent.

The Falcon 50 passengers mumbled something about "Grande Bretagne" and "Cornichons" under their breath. Hollingsworth resisted the temptation to mention, in his best French, that he wished them luck with the plummeting Euro. Britain had retained the Pound Sterling currency throughout their dalliance with the Common Market, and thanks to their ties with the USA it had regained its value after the BREXIT ordeal.

"See you at the booth tomorrow Phil". Hollingsworth said to the passenger closest to him. They had all introduced themselves in the boarding area at Blackbushe airport near the Guilford Campus. But, during the forty-five-minute flight to le Bourget, Hollingsworth had forgotten all their names.

"It's Henry, Henry Forsyth"

"Sorry Henry, I am terrible at names. I'll see you tomorrow."

While his fellow passengers went to get their baggage, Hollingsworth went directly to customs and immigration. He presented his passport and carry-on bag.

"Je n'ai rien a declaré" he said with an authoritative air and perfect French accent

"Bienvenue en France monsieur!" said the agent tipping his hat to Hollingsworth and waved him through. Hollingsworth strode through the exit gate, texting Uber for a ride to the hotel as he went. Hollingsworth had put his baggage in with the shipment of the huge display booth which had arrived at the exhibition hall on the previous day. His hand luggage contained only enough for an overnight stay, so he could collect his baggage the next day. He liked to travel light.

The Uber driver arrived in an Alfa Romeo four-door sedan. He pulled up to the curb next to Hollingsworth, who held up the yellow paddle he always carried with him for this purpose. He had experienced too many cases where his taxi or Uber car had been hijacked by another arriving passenger at a busy airport. He got into the back seat of the car.

"Pas de baggage?" asked the driver.

"Non merci. Hotel Renaissance s'il vous plait... Rue de Mont Thabor." There were several Renaissance hotels in Paris. Some of them were very old and the owners hadn't done much in the way of "renaissance". Hollingsworth tried to avoid them.

They left the airport passing the huge Musee de l'Air et de l'Espace on the right, a huge monolithic building with three 1960's-era Dassault Mirage fighter aircraft mounted on pylons. Each aircraft was pointed skyward at an incongruous angle. The museum had been undergoing renovation since the last airshow which had taken place two years earlier.

The driver took the N2 out of the airport and merged onto the A1, known as the AutoRoute Du Norde. It was known to most commuters as the Auto Parc du Norde. They merged onto the N1 and the driver indicated that he was taking the Route Peripherique around Paris.

"Non, non!" demanded Hollingsworth. "Prendre la Rue de la Chappelle s'il vous plait" The driver shrugged and made a gesture with his hands as only the French can do. He canceled the car's indicator light and continued straight ahead. The Rue de la Chappelle was the more direct route to the Hotel but went through the heart of Paris. It would probably take 10 minutes longer, but Hollingsworth loved Paris and had not been in the city since the previous Airshow. He loved the architecture, the bustling people, the aromas from the coffee shops and restaurants. He even loved to drive in the crazy traffic. It took guts and lightning reflexes to drive in Paris and he had both. The Uber driver... well, not so much.

They turned left on the Rue de Rivoli and went around the block to the hotel. Hollingsworth promised himself that he would take a walk through the Jardin des Tuileries in the early morning. Peter had told him that Marlene, the girl from the office, had asked him where Andrew would be staying. Hollingsworth wondered if she would join him for a walk. Probably not a good idea, he thought to himself. Office romances were severely frowned upon since the #metoo upheaval in the USA. But, he thought, it would be nice to have somebody's hand to hold in one of the most romantic places in Paris.

Hollingsworth gave the driver a fat tip and thanked him for taking the longer route.

"Merci monsieur, Bonne Chance!" The driver was already searching his iPhone for his next ride.

The hotel lobby was packed. Arabs, Chinese, Indians, Brits and a few Americans lined four- deep at the registration desk. Hollingsworth looked around for the concierge, who was talking to a strikingly-dressed colored woman who, he guessed, was from Nigeria.

When the woman moved away, the concierge looked up at him and said, in perfect English," Hello, Mr. Hollingsworth. It's nice to see you again. What can I do for you?"

Hollingsworth wasn't surprised that the concierge knew him. He had been coming to the Paris Air Show for 10 years and usually stayed at this same hotel. The man had worked there for twenty years. He was British.

"Hello George" replied Hollingsworth; "It's good to be back in Paris. Could you hang onto this bag for me and get it over to registration when things slow down a bit. They can leave it in my room. I just don't want to cart it around with me."

"No problem sir, just come back to my desk to get your room keys when you get back."

George took the bag and stowed it behind his desk. Hollingsworth set off toward the Vendor registration desk, which was located on the third floor. By the time he had obtained his credentials, it was 4 p.m. He decided to take a look at how the company's booth was coming along and pick up the remainder of his luggage. It was quite a walk to the exhibition center and he was beginning to worry that the troops may have gone home.

He found the booth, which, he was surprised to find, was much smaller than the one they had at the last show. The company normally booked a corner and took up nine booth spaces, each of which was three meters square.

This year they had three units on the end, with one booth extending down each aisle to form a "U" shape. The booth itself was an all-new design featuring a small glass office where the salespeople could have a quiet conference with clients. It looked better and he assumed that the management had decided to spend a little money on the booth itself and a bit less on renting the space. On reflection, Hollingsworth thought that was a smart decision. The booth had looked a bit shabby at the previous show, and Hollingsworth could not help feeling that it reflected the state of BAE's product line.

The BAE booth was empty. The booth assembly crew had probably gone back to the hotel for a drink and dinner. The end of the adjacent aisle was taken up with a nice booth housing a French industry magazine called "La Defense Electronique". They were one of the many sponsors of the show. An attractive woman wearing jeans, with high heels and a T-shirt with the Eiffel tower emblazoned in gold on the front, was standing on a small ladder adjusting the lights. She was obviously having trouble reaching up to the light fixture.

"Need a hand," asked Hollingsworth as he approached.

The woman turned toward him and Hollingsworth's attention was immediately drawn to her beautiful green eyes. She looked to be in her late thirties, with short dark hair and a soft Mediterranean complexion. He guessed she was French or maybe Algerian. He was surprised that he found himself immediately attracted to her.

"Oh! Thank you, do you mind?" She spoke quietly with a very soft French accent in a voice that somehow resonated with him. She got down from the ladder and handed him the light bulb. He stepped up on the ladder and was easily able to reach the light fixture and insert the bulb which lit up as soon as he screwed it in.

"Could you do the rest for me, please? There are only five more." She smiled up at him and laughed, her eyes shining in the light of the lamp that he had just inserted. Her laugh was infectious. There was a glow about this woman that immediately warmed him. He hadn't experienced an attraction like this for any woman since he had first met Iris. He had been only 21 years old then.

He stepped down from the ladder and she extended her hand to introduce herself.

"Nicole." She said. "Nicole Batault. I am the editor of this boring little magazine.

"Hollingsworth" he replied feeling a bit mesmerized. "Andrew Hollingsworth, I work for BAE," he said pointing to the booth across the aisle with his thumb." She looked in the direction of his thumb and he realized he was pointing in the wrong direction. She had bewitched him completely. She laughed again and he pointed in the other direction, feeling like a schoolboy on a first date.

They worked together for about half an hour. She moved the ladder and handed him the Bulbs, and he screwed them into the fixtures and aimed them in the direction she told him. When they were all done, they stood together in the aisle looking at the booth.

"That looks great!" She said. "Thank you so much, Andrew. Can I buy you a beer or something?"

"I think the kiosk is already closed. Most people have already gone home. There is a little bistro not far from here if you want to try that?" He was nervous now that she might say no.

"D'accord" she responded immediately. He felt his heart skip a beat. What the hell is the matter with me, he thought to himself? Nicole collected her red coat from the back of the booth and they left the exhibition hall through the rear entrance. They walked the few blocks to the bistro and sat down at a corner table.

"I am ravenous," she said, rolling the "r" with a throaty French accent.

"Could we eat?" she asked "Mon petit cadeau pour tout ton travail." offering to buy.

"Of course" he nodded smiling at her. He began to relax and enjoy the warmth of this captivating woman's company. They ordered a glass of wine; she ordered Croque Monsieur and he a traditional French Jambon Beurre. She wolfed down her meal barely talking at all.

"You really were hungry, weren't you?" asked Hollingsworth chuckling. They chatted over their coffee. She told him where she lived and how she had managed to get into the magazine business and how she loved her "fabulous" job. He talked about his job, how things were stagnating at BAE and how much he loved Paris. She asked how long he had been widowed and he told her about Iris' gravesite he had just visited with Peter.

She laughed. That caught him by surprise and somehow turned a morbid moment into a shared memory. She paid the bill and they walked back toward the Exhibition Hall.

"Where are you staying," Nicole asked.

"At the Renaissance, in Paris. Show Headquarters." He replied.

"Me too! Do you need a lift?" He told her he had walked and thought about walking back. But he knew he would rather enjoy a little more time with her. He got in the car.

"Do you have to be at the booth early in the morning to finish setting up?" he asked, and then before she could answer, he said. "I want to take a walk along the Tuileries in the morning. I love that place and I know I won't get time to do that once the show gets started. Would you join me?"

"I'd love to," she said. They parked in the underground garage and took the elevator up to the lobby. He had this incredible urge to kiss her but didn't. He stopped to pick up his keys from the concierge and she smiled at him again.

"Good night Andrew. I'll see you down here at about eight"

"Bon nuit, Nicole" he replied.

Hollingsworth went to his room and started working on his presentation again. "Death by PowerPoint," he thought to himself opening his laptop. "If presentation software development had kept up with weapons development, I would be able to give this talk by thought transfer while lying in my bed." He opened a bottle of beer from the mini-bar in his room and got down to work. It was 11:30 before he finished. He set his alarm for 6:30, got undressed and got into bed. In the blissful few minutes between being awake and sleeping, he thought about Nicole.

The next morning Hollingsworth got up refreshed. He had breakfast in the huge baroque dining room and opened up his laptop in order to make some changes to his presentation. He had decided to face the issues of the fading popularity of the BAE product head-on. He was going to address the issues of the supply and performance of the integrated circuits that go into all the IFF products on the market. He would focus on the projected performance of future products without being specific about who was developing them. He didn't have any commitments from his management that BAE would fund any development. But he didn't care. He had the storyline firmly engraved in his mind now. It was time for that walk.

Nicole was waiting for him in the lobby. She was wearing jeans and walking shoes in favor of the high heels. A white roll-neck sweater contrasted the fitted red tailored coat. Her red wool mittens matched the color of her coat perfectly. A French Blue beret pulled down over her ears completed her outfit. Hollingsworth was completely enchanted.

"Bon jour! Sa va?" she asked taking his arm and heading toward the door.

"I'm good! Did you sleep well?" before she could reply Hollingsworth started telling her about his thoughts on his upcoming presentation and that he was feeling a lot more positive about it. He realized he was babbling on. She smiled up at him letting go of his arm as they left the hotel through the revolving door. They turned right on Rue D'alger, crossed the Rue de Rivoli and entered the park.

They strolled casually down gravel pathway of the Terrace de Feullants, looking at the statues and the huge Mansard roofed buildings along the Rue de Rivoli. There was something satisfying about the crunch of the gravel underfoot. He took her hand in his without thinking. She let go immediately. He felt rejected momentarily but she removed her woolen mitten and, taking his hand again, interlaced her fingers with his. They walked all the way to the Pyramid at the Louvre holding hands and exchanging small talk.

"We'd better start back," Andrew said regrettably. "I have to be at the BAE booth by noon"

"Me too," she said quietly "Thank you for asking me to come along! It's been really nice"

She took his arm again and they walked back to the hotel. In the lobby, she stood on her tiptoes and kissed him superficially on both cheeks, as is the French custom, then backed away from him holding his hand until their arms were both stretched out. Then she let go and hurried off to the elevator

"A bientot!" she said over her shoulder. He blew a kiss to her but she didn't see it.

"God, I think I'm in love!" Hollingsworth said to himself. George passed him on the way to the elevator and asked him how he was.

"I'm in love!" he said to George laughing. George laughed back and winked at him. Hollingsworth went back to his room to collect his laptop and signed on to Uber on his phone. He had to wait 30 minutes for a pick-up. He went down to the lobby to wait.

When he got to the booth there were half a dozen people working on the setup.

"Morning Henry," He got the name right this time. "How is it going?"

"Not good right now Andrew, we can't get the simulators to talk to each other."

For demonstrations, BAE had set up two flight simulators. They both looked like the cockpits of jet fighters. This year, one was the latest British Typhoon and the other an American Raptor. They were very realistic, with a full panel and an ejector seat for the pilot just like the real thing. After an incident at the first show, they took out the cannon shell that fires the ejector seat.

The Typhoon was equipped with the latest BAE weapons systems. While one customer sat in the Typhoon, the other could fly the Raptor on an intercept at any speed with weapons of their choice. The Typhoon "Pilot" could get a first-hand experience of how the system worked. Most of the customers who came to the booth were engineers with no flight training. Many of them had major problems "keeping the blue side up". Andrew always felt that far too many people came to the booth just to fly the simulators and not to buy the product. But it was always fun and over the years he learned all kinds of cool ways to fool his own invention.

He and Henry started a methodical process to find the problem. It took several hours to find a bent pin in one of the miniature D-sub connectors. Some new swearwords were invented during the process. While they were working, Hollingsworth noticed Nicole stroll by, looking for him, so he went to the bathroom to freshen up and strolled over to Defense Electronique's booth.

Nicole was unpacking boxes of magazines while a young man, with long hair and tiny rimless glasses was, hanging posters of mean-looking military aircraft. Smaller posters showed heads-up displays with silhouettes of aircraft caught in the crosshairs of radar gun sites. These were images of modern warfare, remote and terrifying.

"Hello again"

She looked up at him and smiled. She wore the same jeans and what looked like a man's dress shirt which was far too big. She was sweating. She closed her eyes and pursing her lower lip, she blew a wisp of hair away that had fallen over her eyes.

"I was looking for you earlier but you seemed to be very busy. I could hear a lot of cussing going on. Everything OK?" She raised her eyebrows.

"All sorted now" replied Andrew, taking an empty box from her and putting it down with others that were stacked in the booth. Nicole introduced the skinny young man with the tiny glasses.

"This is Joel, he's one of our photographers"

They shook hands and made small talk for a few minutes.

"Got time for a coffee?" he asked Nicole

"Great idea. But I have to freshen up a bit first. I'll meet you over there in a few minutes." She turned to Joel and asked him to flatten down the boxes and take them over to the storage area. Hollingsworth noticed that she was definitely in charge. She had a simple air of authority without being demanding.

Hollingsworth chose a table in the back corner of the coffee shop set up against one wall of the exhibition space. He ordered two coffees and was checking his email when Nicole came in. She had fixed her hair and put some lipstick on.

"i ordered you a café au lait. That ok?"

"Perfect," she said plunking herself down in the chair opposite him. They chatted easily, like old friends, about the day's events and the challenges facing them before the end of the day. They laughed a lot and any observer would get the impression that they were in love.

Her phone buzzed and she took it out of her shirt pocket to check the message. She reached over and put her hand on Andrews, making eye contact.

"I've got to go Andrew, sorry. We have a pre-opening dinner with the whole gang tonight so I won't see you until tomorrow. Let's have dinner if you're free."

With that, she left. He ordered another cup of coffee. When he got back to the booth, Henry had put all the covers back on the simulator panels and they were ready to go.

"Come on Henry, let's do battle!" Henry got into the Typhoon and Hollingsworth took the seat in the Raptor. Henry was a product evaluator. He always managed to beg, borrow or steal examples of competitor's systems so that he could compare their performance with BAEs products in various situations. He flew the simulators a lot. He was smiling now.

They took off from two different airfields that were 500 kilometers apart in the simulated airspace and Hollingsworth soon had Henry on his radar. He was busy flying the airplane, simulating 700 knots, just below the speed of sound. He pressed the button to arm his missiles. It took a few seconds for the green lights to come on, indicating that the weapons were ready.

Henry armed his virtual air-to-air missiles before he took off. In real life, this was a risky tactic since they would likely explode if the aircraft crashed on take-off. But the simulators rarely crashed on take-off and the weapons were virtual anyway. Henry turned on his Identification-Friend or Foe (IFF) system as the plane left the ground. It began sweeping the sky around him sending out a radar signal and searching for an echo. As soon as Andrew's Raptor came within range, the IFF system received the response, analyzed the data in the radar signal and identified the Raptor as a foe.

Henry's display immediately showed the raptor on his display and flashed FOE on the screen. Henry didn't hesitate, firing his first missile immediately. A second later the missile showed on Hollingsworth's screen and all hell broke loose in the cockpit. Alarms went off in Hollingsworth's headset; red lights flashed everywhere and the word "MISSILE" blinked twice per second on the radar screen. Hollingsworth released metal chaff from his aircraft. The chaff offers a larger brighter target to the missile which follows the chaff instead of the enemy plane. That is how it's supposed to work, anyway.

Hollingsworth pulled back hard on the stick and banked hard to the left in a violent evasive maneuver. Had he been flying a real plane, he would have blacked out even if he had been wearing a G-suit. But it was too late. The missile exploded a meter away from his plane and his screen went black.

"Bang you're dead," said Henry with a big grin.

They flew a few more missions and Henry beat him every time except the last mission. On that mission, Andrew managed to fire first. But Henry dived for the ground at Mach 1.5 as soon as the MISSILE warning flashed on his screen. Seconds later, when the missile caught up with him, he was only fifty feet above the ground, traveling at over 1000 miles per hour. The missile, going over 2500 miles per hour couldn't pull out of the dive quite so quickly and hit the ground behind the Typhoon.

"I guess you're buying the beer," said Henry.

"I am," said Andrew. "That was a cool evasion tactic. I will have to remember that one!"

They left the crew to finish up the booth and took a cab back to the hotel. The bar was full of people with the same idea. Marlene from the office was sitting at a table with two men from BAE. She beckoned Hollingsworth over to join them. Henry waved to her and ushered Andrew in the direction of her table. It was obvious that Marlene and her friends were on their second, maybe, third drink.

"So, where have you been hiding Andrew? I have been looking for you since yesterday." Marlene struck a coquettish pose, her drink in one hand and an unlit cigarette in the other.

Andrew turned away to signal the cocktail waitress and said, over his shoulder,

"Henry and I were trouble-shooting the simulators. What did you want me for?"

The other two men at the table chuckled into their beer.

"I think she needs your body" one of the men shouted over the noise of the bar, laughing.

Hollingsworth nodded to Henry and pointed at an empty beer glass on the table. Henry nodded and gave him a thumbs-up.

"Deux bierre si'l vous plait" then asked the others. "Anybody else need anything?"

The waitress bent over so she could hear Hollingsworth. The two guys were staring at the waitress's cleavage, smiling. Hollingsworth shouted his order again.

"Deux bierres Si'l vous plait. C'est tout"

Marlene finally gave up waiting for a sign of chivalry from her male companions and lit her own cigarette. She introduced the two men she was sitting with. Hollingsworth introduced Henry and the conversation soon drifted to the day's work, the issues with the hotel rooms and how long it had taken to get through airport security at Heathrow.

Henry was the first to leave followed quickly by the other two men. Marlene immediately moved to the seat next to Hollingsworth. She leaned on him and spoke so close to his ear that he could feel her breath.

"Where are you taking me for dinner, I am ravenous." Marlene didn't roll her Rs and wore cheap perfume. She had used so much, it was overpowering. Hollingsworth leaned away.

"I have to go too I'm afraid, Marlene. I have to deliver a presentation tomorrow and I haven't even started on it yet" he lied.

"I'll see you tomorrow," he said and left her holding another unlit cigarette.

The next morning Hollingsworth was woken up by his iPhone alarm. He hit the snooze button and lay on his back for a few minutes just staring at the ornate ceiling of his room. He ordered breakfast in the room and took a shower. By the time the meal came, he was dressed in his standard "presentation uniform": a dark business suit, a white shirt with no tie, and black sneakers. Nobody wore ties ever since Steve Jobs passed away many years ago.

He went over the presentation again on his laptop while he ate his breakfast, which consisted of two soft boiled eggs and soldiers; (fingers of buttered toast which you dip into the egg yolk). The coffee was horrible. He caught the shuttle bus to the Conference Center. A few people were already sitting in Room 401 when he arrived. A few were standing in the doorway chatting. Hollingsworth knew many of them.

"Hello Hans, good to see you" to one of the German contingent.

"Hi Earl. It's been a while. What's new?" to an American customer.

"I hope you are here to tell us that", joked the American.

Hollingsworth worked the familiar group for a few minutes and then took his place at the podium. He shuffled papers and tested the PA system hoping for a bigger audience to show up. At ten minutes after the assigned start time he began speaking to an audience of about 20 people;

"Ladies and Gentlemen..."

He introduced himself as the "Product Manager" for BAE's IFF system, even though his title was "Director" and he had responsibility for a wide range of BAE's products. He had found, through experience that downplaying one's real authority made it easier to answer questions regarding the company's strategy with which he often disagreed.

He opened by facing BAE's product shortcomings head-on. The bottom line was that the product was too slow to be effective in the modern aerial battlefield. Furthermore, it lacked some of the features of its competitors. In particular, it required pilots to enter codes each day. This was recognized as being a key source of human error, with potentially disastrous results.

Hollingsworth then outlined the features and performance he thought were required to meet the demands of future aerial warfare. He went into some detail on the need for speed; He talked about new developments by the companies that produced the microprocessors for the current system. He spoke specifically about the need for secure sources of all components. He mentioned the Japanese supplier Subiki, which was the only source of the fastest integrated circuits, and pointed out that their production capacity was limited. He made it clear that the speed of the aircraft and accuracy of the missiles today meant that the first to fire wins the battle. To be the first to fire, you have to have the fastest IFF system. This means the electronics have to be able to sweep the enemy aircraft, obtain a response and identify the target as a friend or foe faster than the enemy aircraft's system can identify you,

He discussed the need for automatic software updates and secure interfaces to various military networks. He also showed a couple of slides outlining the need for easy "swap-and-go" maintenance, including the ability to clone set-up information when units were replaced. This had been a constant source of problems at BAE.

He outlined the need for a simpler interface to current and future weapon aiming and firing systems like Heads-up Displays and Virtual Reality helmets. Hollingsworth never mentioned or even suggested that BAE was working on any of these features. He noticed Joel sitting at the back of the room taking notes.

The question and answer period was brutal. The Saudi Arabian Government, which had bought 50 new Typhoon fighters from BA only three years before, was angry. The aircraft had come equipped with the BAE IFF system at that time with promises of upgrades within 6 months. After the revolution in Saudi Arabia, the country had made a pact with the UIA and they wanted the systems upgraded immediately. Hollingsworth knew that wasn't going to happen.

Hollingsworth finally had to admit that he didn't know when BAE would be able to ship the upgraded systems. It all depended on the supply and performance of the integrated circuits being supplied by Subiki.

After the presentation, Hollingsworth was collecting his papers together when one of the people who had been in the audience, came up to him.

"Hi, I'm Jack Husher I run a small venture capital firm in California. We specialize in funding companies that design and produce electronic products for the military. I was impressed by your presentation this morning. You are the first person I've heard that has honestly spelled out what the upcoming issues are with these products."

Hollingsworth shook hands with the man, who had short curly hair with a sprinkling of grey. He had a pleasant twinkle in his eye which put people at ease. He had a definite Pittsburgh accent. Hollingsworth smiled;

"Thank you. I just try to convey the facts. Unfortunately, the facts are that right now most of this stuff isn't fast enough to be effective against the kind of weapons we have available today."

"Do you think that BAE will be able to fix that problem in the near future?" asked Husher.

"As I said, I think that depends on the availability and performance of the new chips that are supposed to be coming on the market."

"Got time for a coffee?" Husher followed Hollingsworth, who had now stuffed all his notes into his briefcase and had started toward the exit.

"No. I don't have time right now I'm afraid; it's my turn in the booth. Sorry about that."

The fact was that Hollingsworth needed a stiff drink. They talked for a few more minutes and Husher gave him his business card. They agreed to meet for dinner that evening. Hollingsworth had forgotten that he had a dinner date with Nicole that evening.

Hollingsworth made his way back to his hotel room and got changed into the monogrammed blue golf shirt and khaki pants that made up the booth "uniform". He went out and got a single glass of ice from the machine in the corridor and poured one of the miniature bottles of Black Label over it. He grabbed the remote, lay back on the bed and turned the TV on.

"Thank God that's over," he said to himself knocking back the scotch in one gulp. He switched the TV to a cartoon channel.

He had been asleep for nearly an hour when his mobile rang. It was Henry .

"Where the fuck are you Andrew? I am starving and need you here to relieve me at the booth!"

"On my way" replied Andrew, getting up.

When he got to the booth Henry was sitting in the Raptor. An American whom Hollingsworth knew was sitting in the Typhoon simulator.

"Hello Earl." Hollingsworth nodded at the American. Then to Henry, he said "I'll take it from here Henry, go get some lunch."

"About time! How did it go this morning?" asked Henry.

"Brutal" replied Hollingsworth "Brutal!"

Hollingsworth played fighter pilots with Earl for a while then Earl got out of the cockpit, thanking Hollingsworth as he left. "See you later Earl"

Hollingsworth went into the office to check the bulletin board and get his messages. One message was from Jack Husher. It said "Andrew, see you tonight in the lobby at seven" It was signed by Jack. The second message was in an envelope with the "Defense Electronique" logo printed on it and his name typed: "Andrew Hollingsworth". He opened it to find a small slip of paper with the message "Tu me manqué", written by hand and signed with a flourish "N".

Hollingsworth smiled to himself. "She's missing me ... that's nice"

He suddenly realized that he was supposed to have dinner with Nicole that evening and had just agreed to meet with Jack Husher at seven.

"Damn," he said to himself.

Henry came back with the smell of beer on his breath. Hollingsworth told him about the presentation and the hard time the Saudis had given him.

"Assholes," said Henry. "I can't believe they hitched up with that rabid load of Muslims."

"No, I can't either but they all hate the USA and want to annihilate Israel." Hollingsworth picked his messages up off the desk and asked Henry

"It's gone pretty quiet now, can you hold the fort for a bit"

"Sure," said Henry

Hollingsworth strolled over to Nicole's booth. Three Saudis wearing traditional white thobes with a red and white checkered ghutra were standing at the booth. He stood a discreet distance away until they left.

"I got your message," he said. "So I came over right away. Are you really missing me?"

"I am" she replied, taking his arm and looking up into his eyes. "I can't wait until dinner."

"I'm afraid I am going to have to stand you up tonight Nicole. Jack Husher wants me to have dinner with him. I think he is going to offer me a job."

"You're standing me up? That's it! It's all over!" she teased him, her tone harsh, and her eyes soft. "That's ok," she said "I have to go over some stuff with Joel tonight anyway. I've written a short piece on your presentation for the special show issue of the magazine. We have to wrap up the magazine for print by midnight."

"Yes, I saw Joel taking notes…. Tomorrow night then?" Hollingsworth asked hesitantly.

"Can't wait!" she said pecking him on one cheek.

He drew her back to him and kissed her quickly on the lips.

"Nor me," he said holding her just a little longer than necessary.

Jack Husher was waiting for him in the lobby at precisely seven p.m. They ate in a discreet corner booth in the hotel dining room. It was early, and, at first, they had the huge room and a bevy of waiters to themselves.

After some small talk and a couple of cocktails, Husher gave Andrew a thick manila envelope.

"This is a prospectus I am about to put out for a company I am funding to produce Defense Electronics for the American and Allied market. I don't expect to have much trouble raising the $20 million we need to get it off the ground. I want you on the team as Chief Engineer. I want you to read this and give me an answer before the Paris Air Show ends. There is a healthy salary and benefits package which is quite a bit better than the pittance that BAE is paying you. But you will have to move to the States, the San Francisco Bay area that is. We'll get you work visas and take care of moving expenses and all the logistics. You will get 10% of the initial stock offering. You can do the math."

Hollingsworth was dumbfounded. He had been expecting some overtures to work in the USA but this was a dream come true. This was a chance to design and build his own product line with proper funding and, he suspected, a lot fewer politics.

Hollingsworth didn't open the package. The two talked for two hours about their own backgrounds. Husher had been an innovator in the Semiconductor industry at its height in the 70s and 80s. He made a lot of money and went into semi-retirement funding what he called "worthy causes for our military". This had included funding the development of a mobile field operating room that was deployed with huge success in the Iraq war and later in Afghanistan. Most of those funds, it was rumored, came out of Husher's own pocket.

More recently he had helped Litton Industries get funds appropriated for two huge defense projects. Husher certainly knew all the right people. But what struck Hollingsworth was Husher's clear honesty and patriotic motivation. He would do anything he could for his country.

The two men shook hands warmly and parted company.

"I'll read this and get back to you Jack. I can tell you right now that this is an interesting proposition." Inwardly, Hollingsworth had already made up his mind without reading the small print. He liked Husher, it was a terrific compensation deal, and San Francisco wasn't a terrible place to live. Compared to Guilford….

He couldn't wait to tell Nicole and he wanted to see her. He called her room. He knew it wasn't the proper thing to do but he was so excited that he couldn't resist.

"Allo." Nicole answered with an impatient tone in her voice. Hollingsworth caught the tone immediately and decided that his news could wait.

"Just wanted to say good night," he said quietly, wishing he hadn't made the call.

"That's sweet, Andrew thanks. But I really have to go, we are only 45 minutes from the deadline and we are not ready."

"OK. See you tomorrow night" he said and hung up.

The next morning Hollingsworth went for a walk in the Tuileries. It was cold for late June in Paris and he walked only halfway, stopping for a coffee and a croissant at a small Tabac.

By the time he got to the booth, it was ten o'clock. The booth was bustling with people, mostly Arabs. When the crowd waned, Hollingsworth spent some time with Henry. They talked about the way Henry had avoided the missiles in the last demonstration they had flown together.

"That was pretty quick-thinking Henry," said Hollingsworth

"Not really. There are some new tactics evolving that work. That tactic worked that time, but generally, if a missile locks on you are better off ejecting. That's if you have time to eject!"

Henry went on to explain the flight characteristics of current missiles. "Basically," he said "the faster they fly, the wider their turn rate. If you can out-turn the missile you have a chance. But you have to detect it first. If it's too close before you detect it, you're history. It's that simple. I saw the missile you fired almost immediately. I dived for the deck knowing I could pull out of the dive but the missile probably wouldn't. I have tried that trick about 10 times on the simulator and that's the first time it worked. So, the odds aren't that good. In real life, I'd eject"

Hollingsworth and Henry took a walk around the booths in their exhibition Hall. They stopped and asked a few awkward questions at Litton and a couple of other competitor's booths. It was the custom at the shows. Everybody knew everybody else in this narrow industry. Most of the engineers would wind up working for most of the Companies during their careers. The Paris Airshow was always like "old home week".

At four o'clock Hollingsworth helped the crew clean up the booth and prepare for the next day. Marlene gave Hollingsworth a very cold shoulder and left the Hall with Earl,

the American. Hollingsworth bought Henry a beer in the hotel bar and went to collect his messages from the lobby. Another envelope from "Defense Electronique" was in his box. He opened it and took out the slip of paper.

"Dinner 7:30 p.m. No excuses! I made the reservation already!
It was signed simply "N".

Hollingsworth grinned and went up to his room. He flipped on
the TV and opened up the prospectus that Jack Husher had
given him the previous evening. It was 15 pages of legalese
advising against investing in such a risky project. He was asleep
by the end of page 4.

The alarm on his iPhone woke him up at six o'clock. He
showered and shaved and tried to decide what to wear. He had
only brought business attire and his booth "uniform". He
hadn't expected to be going out on a dinner date. He settled for
khaki pants and a white dress shirt. He could wear his blazer if it
was cold.

Nicole was waiting for him in the lobby when he went down.
She was wearing a classic "little black dress" with spaghetti
straps and black pumps with three-inch heels. She was
carrying a short jacket and the tiniest handbag he had ever
seen. She was stunningly elegant.

"Bon Soir!" she said quickly taking his arm.

They walked outside.

"C'est en peu nippy," she said, giving Andrew her jacket so that
he would help her put it on. He helped her on with her jacket
and decided to put on his blazer.

"Thanks," she said. "Uber is on the way"

It took a few minutes for the car to arrive and he put his arm
around her shoulders to keep her warm. When the car arrived,

she spoke to the driver in French. "Le Palais du Bourget s'il vous plait. Prendre le Rue Gilbert "and then to Andrew, she said. "I asked him to take us through town. It's beautiful in the evening and it's a funky little town." They settled back in the comfortable car and she took his hand.

"Tell me everything!" she said.

Hollingsworth told her what Husher had said almost verbatim. He explained that according to the prospectus, Husher was funding a new company to compete in the Military Avionics industry. He had substantial funding available and wanted him on the team. "It seems that they will do it with or without me, but they are giving me the first right of refusal regarding the engineering job. It's a dream come true if it's real."

He didn't have to explain to Nicole that 10% of $20,000,000 was two million dollars. Nicole was quick to point out that it wasn't cash. It was stock and it would only be worth two million if the company actually succeeded and made the financial goals outlined in the prospectus. She was quick to point out that there was a lot of risk involved. Her own magazine had very nearly failed in the first year and she had to give up a lot more equity to get more funding. "There's a reason they call them 'Vulture Capitalists' you know," she said, with a certain bitterness in her voice.

They arrived at the restaurant. It looked Chinese with a classic glazed green tile roof. It was warm inside and the Maitre de' offered to take her jacket. They were seated in a corner table for two. The building had obviously been a large home at one time and each room had been altered to accommodate a few tables for two to four people. The furnishings and décor served to muffle the noise and the candles on each table lent an ambience to the place, as well as a romantic setting.

Hollingsworth ordered two Kir-Royals, an old-fashioned drink made with Champagne and Crème de Cassis. Nicole smiled inwardly. It was one of her favorite drinks.

Hollingsworth continued on about the meeting with Husher but she interrupted him quickly.

"No more business talk," she said "Now I want to know about you." She reached across the table and took his hand under hers. Her eyes shone in the flickering candlelight.

"Did anybody ever tell you what lovely eyes you have?" he asked.

"Yes, several people have" she laughed. "Now tell me about you. I want to know everything about you. Le Tout!" she laughed again.

He began with his career. He told her that he had always wanted to be a pilot. While still in high school, he had taken the entrance examinations to get into Cranfield (the Royal Airforce Academy) and had passed with flying colors but failed the eyesight test. He told her about how his father had always wanted him to become an apprentice. "After I failed the eyesight test, I moped around for months doing nothing. I didn't get a job and didn't apply to go to college. My Dad arranged for me to be interviewed at the Bristol Airplane company for an apprenticeship. He drove me down there, about 200 miles. I told the guy who was interviewing me that if the apprenticeship was the last job on the planet, I wouldn't take it. He got really angry and told my father, who drove off and left me there. I had to hitchhike home."

"You're kidding," she said.

"No" I replied. "At one point around that time, my father thought I was gay."

"Seriously? Tell me more." She was now looking at him very intently.

"It's a long story," Andrew said and ordered two more Kirs.

"Go on," she said.

"When I was in Grammar School, I had a friend named Graham Rowley. We were joined at the hip from the first day of Grammar school when I was 12 until the day he left to go to Cambridge University.

"We used to ride our bicycles past the local junkyard twice a day, once on the way to school and once on the way home. The wooden perimeter fence around the yard was dilapidated from years of neglect. Boards were missing or loose, making it easy for us skinny kids to sneak into the yard. Graham and I nearly always stopped to explore. There was always something new to see since the yard was close to the new motorway, and wrecks from the numerous accidents would often wind up in the yard. Graham and I both had a morbid curiosity about the mangled cars with smashed windshields and black stains on the seats. We would recreate the accidents in our vivid imagination."

"Anyway, there was an old guy named Joe that looked after the yard. He only had one eye and always wore the same pair of baggy pants tied around his waist with a piece of rope. The story was that he lost an eye when he was installing the guns in a Spitfire at the end of WWII and a cartridge hit him in the face and took his eye out. He had a gammy leg and couldn't run fast enough to catch a cold so we never took much notice him."

The waiter brought the drinks and asked if they were ready to order. Nicole asked him to give her a few more minutes.

"Anyway, it turned out that he used to ride in the TT races on the Isle of Man. When we found an old bike in the yard, he helped us get it running and taught us how to ride it. We had to repair that entire fence first but we learned a lot. We used to say that if we failed our college exams we could always work as carpenters after that."

"We used to ride the bike along the railway lines an up on the Canal tow-paths. One day I was going too fast and drove into the canal. The engine exploded!" Hollingsworth laughed at the memory of that event. But it wasn't funny at the time."

"Your parents allowed you to do all this?" Nicole asked incredulously.

"They didn't know." Hollingsworth laughed again." We pretended we had girlfriends. We rode the motorbike after school and on the weekends. My Mom thought I had met my soulmate because I was so happy. But I was just having a load of fun with the motorbike."

"So why did your father think you were gay?" Nicole was curious now.

"My father often saw me with Graham but my Mom thought I was with this girl Elizabeth, whom I couldn't stand. We made up a girl for Graham. Her name was Rebecca Rudge. We named her after the bike. It was a Rudge 500 model. My father grew suspicious as this deceit went on all summer. "Well one day, as I said, I was riding the bike way too fast and drove it off the tow-path into the canal. The engine blew up and I had to get dragged out of the canal.   We had to tell the whole story to my Mom and Dad. My Mom fainted I think."

The waiter came and took their order. Hollingsworth ordered a nice bottle of Fumé Blanc to go with the Bouillabaisse they had both ordered. Nicole kept the conversation focused on Andrew while they ate their entree. Then Andrew changed the subject.

"Have you ever flown in a sailplane?" he asked

"You mean, like a glider? No, I haven't"

"Well, the show opens to the public sector tomorrow. We don't do much other than Corporate PR with the public so I am not needed in the booth until we tear down. I was thinking about going down to Saint Auban and doing some flying. Would you like to come with me?"

"This doesn't involve flying upside-down does it?" She laughed. "A Russian pilot offered to take me up tomorrow and get me to join the Mile-High club inverted. I turned him down." she grinned knowingly

"No," said Hollingsworth "but it may involve getting a little high"

They both laughed and continued flirting self-consciously until the waiter arrived with the Bill, which Hollingsworth reluctantly let Nicole pay after she repeatedly told him that it was her treat.

Hollingsworth conceded finally by countering "OK, but I buy the nightcap. I have a nice bottle of Armagnac in my room."

"Mmmmm. That sounds good" she purred as he helped her on with her coat.

On the way back to the hotel, she leaned against him, resting her head against his shoulder. He put his arm around her. She nestled closer like a contented cat. They didn't have to talk.

Hollingsworth paid the driver and they took the elevator to his floor. As soon as the elevator doors closed, he took her in his arms and kissed her tenderly. The sensation was electric. They both felt it and their passion had just begun to rise when the elevator stopped at Hollingsworth's floor and the bell abruptly ended that round.

Hollingsworth opened the door for her and, taking off his blazer, he asked,

"Armagnac, right?"

She nodded. Pouring 40-year-old Armagnac into a plastic cup didn't feel quite right to Hollingworth and, passing the cup to Nicole, he said with a terribly affected British accent,

"Sorry darling, I couldn't find the bloody crystal!"

She didn't get the humor at first and then laughed with him, carefully touching his plastic cup with hers.

"Clink," she said and made herself comfortable sitting up in his bed. She patted the bed, inviting him to join her.

Hollingsworth moved to her side of the bed and took the glass away from her, setting it down on the side table with his own. He began kissing her again. Tenderly at first. Her response quickly turned passionate. She began kissing his neck. She held his face to hers with her hand caressing his face then, her fingers thrust into his hair. She began to probe his mouth with her tongue. With her other hand, she began to undo the buttons of his shirt. She let her fingers trail seductively over his left nipple. He quickly became completely aroused, something that hadn't happened spontaneously for some time.

He began to unbutton her blouse. She lay back on the bed, supplicant. She helped him undo the front clasp of her push up bra and cupped her breasts in her hands, offering her hard nipples to his mouth. Her hand now moved down feeling the heat of his passion through his clothing.

It was his turn to be supplicant now, and he lay back looking at her as she began to undo his belt and unzip his pants. He was completely exposed to her now, unabashed at his naked unbridled passion.

"Mmmmm" she purred, looking down at him. "I need you! But not now. I have to be up at five tomorrow morning and I want to be able to spend an entire night enjoying every inch of your entire body. All of it. All night" she said getting up from the bed.

Saint Auban.

They flew down to Nice and rented a little convertible Renault. Nicole wanted to drive. As they left the airport, Hollingsworth called a number on his mobile contact list.

"Bonjour, Centre National de Vol a Voile" Much to his surprise, a real person answered the phone. He recognized the voice.

"Francois it's Andrew. Did you get my message last night?"

"Yes, I have the ASH25 rigged for you. We are putting some oxygen in it as we speak. I assume you are current in gliders. Do you have your renter's insurance up to date or a $250,000 credit limit on your Visa?"

"Yes, I should be good to go" he laughed. "I am bringing a very beautiful lady from the International Aviation press with me. She might get you some good publicity."

"So long as you don't make her puke like you did that guy from AOPA," Francois laughed.

"He was a jerk. But I promise I won't do that again. You made me clean out the plane, remember?"

"OK. See you in about an hour." Hollingsworth hung up the mobile. He leaned over and kissed Nicole on her neck.

St. Auban housed the French National Soaring club. The French National Soaring Champion worked there as an instructor. The club owned some of the highest-performance gliders in the world. Only a few very experienced pilots were allowed to fly some of them, which cost $300,000 and required a great deal of skill to handle safely.

The airfield is located in French Alps, affording some of the most spectacular (and unforgiving) soaring in the world. Hollingsworth had flown there many times, including flying in

World Sailplane Grand Prix held there in 2005. He finished 5th in a field of 44
competitors from all over the World. When asked by an aviation reporter how he liked flying in the Alps he had responded with one word.

"Terrifying!"

Now mountain flying was his favorite kind of soaring and he flew at Saint Auban a lot. He had introduced quite a few of his ground-bound customers to the joys of soaring when they came to France for the Paris Airshow or on vacation. Few ever forgot the experience. Quite a few British Typhoon pilots who had flown with Hollingsworth at St Auban took up soaring. An American who flew U2s for NASA in California bought a glider a month after flying with Hollingsworth in Saint Auban. The road to Saint Auban from Marseilles goes through the foothills of the Alps. It is a treacherous winding road through some of the most spectacular scenery in France.

Nicole was enjoying the drive on the winding mountain roads, her hair blowing in the wind over the open car. She shifted expertly up and down the gears. The little car didn't have the power of her E-type Jaguar but it was agile and she took the turns with lots of power on. Every now and then the skinny tires would squeal in protest and Hollingsworth would
look up see if they were about to die.

When they got to the airfield the weather was getting warm and a few gliders were getting ready to launch. As editor of a prestigious industry magazine, she had been invited to take flights in a lot of military aircraft. She had experienced aerobatics in a French Dassault Mirage fighter and rode in "a lot" of helicopters. But she wasn't familiar with gliders or "sailplanes" as Hollingsworth always called them.

She was immediately surprised at the wingspan of these beautiful fiberglass works of art. The ASH 25 had a wingspan of 87·5 feet - almost as big as a Boeing 737-100 airliner. The long, tapered wings were less than a meter wide at the cockpit, which looked very similar to that of the Mirage fighter. It was very small with a huge Plexiglas "bubble" canopy that opened in two parts. The canopy over the front seat tilted forward and the rear canopy titled back.

Unlike the fighters she had been in, there was no ejector seat. In fact, both seats reclined like Porsche "Ricaro" car seats. They had five-point seat belts, and lumbar support was provided by little bladders in the seat that could be inflated by a small pump like those used on blood pressure monitors.

Hollingsworth introduced Nicole to Francois.

"Would you give Nicole a cockpit briefing Francois while I go do the paperwork at the Office?"

"Sure," said Francois "Are you going to use the club 'chutes?"

"Yes, please. Show her how to work the radio and the oxygen if you would."

"Ok, let's get your 'chute on first Nicole. Turn around please" Francois held the chute up behind her like a backpack so she could put her arms through the shoulder straps. The leg straps hung down between her legs.

"I'll let you get those straps yourself" grinned Francois.

He demonstrated how to adjust the straps so the chute was comfortable. Then he showed her how the ripcord worked.

"I've worn a 'chute before," she said.

"In the unlikely event then you do have to bail out, cover your head with your hands, jump and count to 10 before you pull the ripcord. This plane has a T-tail as you can see. It the aircraft is spinning you don't want that to hit you in the head. . . OK, let's get you in"

Francois showed Nicole how to get into the front seat. "You sit on the cockpit rail like this with both legs outside the cockpit. Then you swing both feet over the rail. Lift your right leg up over the stick."

She sat on the rail looking up at the instructor.

"Did anybody ever tell you what lovely eyes you have?" said Francois grinning.

"Many times," she responded laughing with the young instructor.

By the time that Hollingsworth got back, Nicole was sitting in the cockpit with her parachute on and seat belts fastened.

"Thanks, Francois" I'll take it from here.

"Comfortable?" Hollingsworth asked. Nicole nodded

Hollingsworth explained how to turn on the radio and change channels. He showed her the yellow knob that released the tow line.

"Don't pull that unless I tell you. Got it?"

"OK, got it"

He turned to Francois

"Have him tow us to 1500 meters"

Hollingsworth got in the back seat of the glider and went through the pre-takeoff checklist printed on a laminated plastic card. He pointed or touched each instrument or control in turn, verifying the correct reading or position. It was quite a long list, considering the plane had no engines.

"Spoilers: closed and locked"

"Canopy: closed and locked"

"Pre-Takeoff checklist complete"

"OK, are you ready to cheat death and gravity, Nicole?"
"I am," she said, "but only with you." He could hear the smile in her voice.

The tow plane took up a position on the runway in front of the glider and Francois came over to connect the tow line to the glider. Hollingsworth spoke into the boom microphone in the rear cockpit:

"Tow plane Glider Zulu Seven Sierra, take up slack"

The engine of the tow plane grew louder and it began to move forward slowly. The tow line snaked along the blacktop until it was taught.

"Launch, launch, launch," said Hollingsworth into the microphone. The single-engine French Rallye tow plane picked up speed quickly, and within a few seconds, the glider was off the ground. Nicole's hands came up and gripped the cockpit side rails.

"Relax," Hollingsworth said softly. "We're good."

Hollingsworth held the plane level about a foot above the blacktop while the Rallye gathered flying speed. At about 110 kilometers per hour, it lifted smoothly into the air and the two aircraft began to climb out of the beautiful Alpine Valley surrounded by snowcapped mountains. BIG snowcapped mountains.

"This is beautiful," said Nicole. "I can see why you enjoy this so much. C'est magnifique, absolutement magnifique"

A few minutes later they were just below the tops of some of the smaller mountains. It seemed that they were headed directly for the rock face. Nicole's hands came up to grip the cockpit rails again. The tow plane made a shallow turn to the left to parallel the mountain face.

"Pull that yellow knob please Nicole." The glider had a yellow release knob in the back seat as well but he wanted Nicole to feel she was participating, not just along for
the ride. She pulled the release and heard a metallic "thunk". She watched the tow rope drop away from the glider and the tow plane make a steep dive back in the direction from which

they had come. Hollingsworth continued to fly toward the mountain face.

"Don't worry we are not going to hit the mountain. When the wind hits that rock face it gets pushed up the slope. As we get closer, we will get pushed up with it."

Right on cue, the glider began to rise up the rock face. Hollingsworth turned right, flying parallel to the rock face about fifty meters away. He followed another glider doing the same thing about 100 meters below them.

"What's that noise?" asked Nicole, suddenly aware of the quiet beeping sound coming from the panel. "It sounds like the microwave popcorn is done" she laughed a bit nervously

"That's the variometer," said Hollingsworth. "It tells us if we are climbing or descending. That round dial on the top right of your panel shows the same thing visually. We are going up about 15 meters per second right now." "Beeping means we are going up and booping means down. The faster and shriller the beep rate, the faster we are climbing. We use the audio vario so we don't have to look down at the panel when we are so close to the terrain. It's not a good idea."

"Merde!" she said. "I can see that" as the rocks flashed by their wingtip at 150 kph. "I've flown as a passenger in the Alps in a jet trainer, but never this low, and it had a billion kilos of thrust whenever they needed it. I had no idea that gliders could do this kind of thing. This IS fun!"

The glider reached the top of the mountain ridgeline and Hollingsworth started flying toward a large puffy white cloud hovering over the end of the ridge. As he approached it, the vario began to beep incessantly.

"I am going to make a steep turn," said Hollingsworth. "Don't be nervous."

Hollingsworth banked the glider over at a 45-degree angle. The beeping rate increased rapidly. They were climbing at 3 meters per second. They soon reached the bottom of the big cloud. It went cold when they were out of the sun. Nicole closed the little vent on the side of the canopy as Francois had shown her. They were already 4000 meters above sea level, way higher than most of the mountains around them. Hollingsworth leveled the wings and flew out over the magnificent valley below them.

"Do you want to fly it? Left stick and left rudder together to turn left. Push forward and the houses get bigger. Pull back and they get smaller"

He loved that old aviator's saw. He made a gentle turn in each direction and then put the nose down gently, pulling up slowly into a graceful turn. The wings arced upward under the strain.

"I'm not sure," said Nicole obviously excited but nervous about the prospect of actually piloting the plane herself.

"Put your toes on the pedals when you are ready" Hollingsworth spoke in a light-hearted tone.

"Ok," He said. "Now hold the stick between your thumb and two fingers. Got it?

"Yes I think so"

"Ok, your airplane. Gently does it"

Within a half-hour, she had the basics and could easily fly the plane straight and level. She made shallow turns really well, but like most beginners, she had a hard time controlling the airspeed in a steep bank. Hollingsworth was impressed. After about half an hour Hollingsworth said

"That's enough for now. Let's head back"

He cranked the plane over into a tight 60-degree bank. Within minutes they were back at 4000 meters above sea level. That was more than enough altitude to get back to St Auban at 150 kph. He put the nose down and snugged up his seat belt.

"Tighten your seat belt. It might get a bit bumpy." Nicole complied. No hands gripping the cockpit rail now.

The sleek glider sliced silently through the mountain air. It was so quiet that it was easy to carry on a conversation at normal volume. No audio headsets were required. The last time Nicole had been in a jet, she couldn't hear for three days afterward.

Hollingsworth called the airport and reported entering the traffic pattern. Landing the huge glider took concentration. The wings were more than three times the width of the runway and the wingtips were a mere half meter above the ground. Speed control was critical. The big glider was heavy. Too fast and he would go off the end of the runway. Too slow and he would hit hard and bounce. He tried to make every landing a precision landing and he touched down within a few feet of his target only a couple of knots over the optimum airspeed. He closed the spoilers and let the plane roll onto the apron still balanced on its single wheel. Francois was there to catch the wingtip.

The temperature in the cockpit rose very rapidly now there was no airflow. Nicole opened her canopy.

"Did you enjoy the ride?" Francois asked Nicole.

"Magnifique" she replied. "I had no idea! I think that is the most enjoyable ride I have ever had in an airplane. He even let me fly it a little bit. I loved it."

Francois helped her get her seat belt unfastened. She sat upright.

"It's easier if you shuck the 'chute first," said Francois. "Just rotate that center buckle and it will release all the straps."

Francois took her hand while she got out of the glider. It was obvious that he really liked her eyes.

Hollingsworth got out of the back seat.

"She's taken!" he said to Francois laughing.

"Merde,," said the young man. "If only I was ten years older!" They all laughed. Francois called the ground crew over to tend to the glider.

Andrew and Nicole walked over to the clubhouse. Several people greeted Hollingsworth as they walked in. He ordered two beers. They sat at a small table with high stools.

"You seem to know everybody in this place." Nicole said after sipping the froth off her beer.

"I guess I do. I have been doing this for a long time."

"You are a good teacher," she said taking his hand in hers.

"Can we stay here tonight? I really hate Marseilles. We could drive back to Paris if you like."

"They have a nice bunkhouse here for the pilots. I get to stay for free if I give instruction." He grinned. He knew what was coming next.

"No way!" she exclaimed. "I want a nice dinner in a nice little place with a fireplace, a bed and you. All to myself!" She was looking into his eyes with a tenderness he had not seen before."

"How can I resist that offer" he replied, leaning over the table and kissing her affectionately on her forehead. "I'll go pay my bill."

The woman behind the counter greeted him.

"Hello Andrew, I heard you were here." Andrew had made friends with the middle-aged Husband-and-wife managers of the Glider club.

"I'm good, what's the damage?" he asked

"She turned to the computer and looked up his bill. 280 Euros" she said.

"How is the Chateau Arnoux in town?" he asked, proffering his credit card.

"It's really nice. It's not cheap though. Who's the nice young lady?" she smiled at him knowingly

"Is the food any good?" he asked, trying to sidestep the question.

"Marc and I have eaten there a couple of times on special occasions. It was marvelous."

She leaned over the counter and in a lower voice said "Come on Andrew you can tell me." She smiled at him again. "Who is she?"

"Her name is Nicole." Hollingsworth blurted out reluctantly

"She is the editor of Defense Eleqtronique, a French Aerospace Industry magazine."

"Impressive!" she said, passing Andrew his receipt.

"She has beautiful eyes," she said, then added "Bonne Chance!"

He called the Chateau Arnoux to book a room. They had only one room with a fireplace, but it was 350 Euros per night. He took it. Nicole was still at the bar when he got back. Francois was chatting her up.

"Ready?" he said taking her coat.

They drove the short distance to the Chateaux and checked in. The concierge arranged to take their bags to their room and they sat in a cozy corner of the lounge and ordered coffee.

"So was Elizabeth your first?" asked Nicole, a naughty inquisitive look on her face.

Hollingsworth holds up both hands in protest. The Maitre d' came and sat them at a table in the corner. The flickering candles on the tables added a romantic ambience to the lovely old dining room. They sat down on the same side of the table.

"Enough about me for now. Now it's your turn. I bet you were a little tomboy, weren't you?"

Hollingsworth filled her wine glass. She conceded.

"I was born in Corsica. My mother was French and my father was Algerian. We moved to Paris when my parents got divorced. I was 13 at the time."

She re-filled her wine glass and Hollingsworth sensed that the conversation was going to become much more serious.

"I had my first boyfriend at 15 and was pregnant at 16. I had an abortion which I regret to this day. My father was killed in Algeria at that time and I had a difficult time dealing with all that."

Hollingsworth reached across the table and took her hand this time.

"I got my Baccalaureate at 17 and went to the Sorbonne on a scholarship. I was determined to make something of my miserable life. I graduated in Accounting & Finance but took a degree in English at the same time. It was easy, because English was my second language. My father didn't speak very good French even though he was brought up in Algeria. That turned out to be a very smart move. My first job was as a junior accounting clerk in the US Embassy in Paris. I worked there for 10 years. That's where I met my husband."

Nicole looked up at Hollingsworth now with a pained expression on her face.

"I'm married, Andrew" she drew her hand away from his and looked down. "I should have told you before. I am sorry." She made eye contact with him again and went on: "I hardly know you Andrew but I feel so totally at ease with you. I can't explain it and I don't really know why. I haven't experienced that before, not even with my husband. I didn't want to spoil that by telling you I was married. I am sorry."

Hollingsworth was stunned. He had guessed she was probably divorced and had been for some time. He felt that the magic balloon he had created around her was about to burst.

"How long have you been married?" was all he could think to say.

"Eleven years." she said. "It was quite good at first. But we moved to Tel Aviv four years ago and things have become progressively more difficult ever since. We are both very strong-willed people and when we fight, we hurt each other emotionally. My husband has a very short fuse. We got in a terrible fight 6 months ago. He got drunk, not something he did regularly, and he hit me. I won't tolerate that. I left and have rented a place from a friend of mine while she is in the USA."

Hollingsworth was silent for a few minutes, trying to grasp the situation and the role he played in it. He was emotionally numb. He didn't say anything for several minutes, trying not to make eye contact with her.

"Are you going to go back to him?" he asked, finally breaking the silence. Hollingsworth wasn't sure he wanted to hear the answer to his question but he had to ask.

"I don't know." She said. She had recovered her composure now and dabbed her eyes with a tissue. Her mascara was badly smudged. "He has been a wonderful husband until recently and he has apologized a hundred times for hitting me. He says it will never happen again."

Hollingsworth thought to himself "They all say that." He thought for a moment about what to say to this woman who, in a matter of a few days, had completely captivated him. He sat for several minutes just staring out of the window. How could this be happening, he asked himself. He could end it now and she may or may not go back to her husband. He wouldn't ever win her heart if he ended it now. And he realized he desperately wanted to win her heart. He realized that he had nothing to lose and that he was going to give up without a fight. It took him a few moments to formulate the words in his mind, then he spoke quietly and assuredly.

"Look, Nicole, I am going to honest with you. I know we have only just met but I haven't felt this close to a woman since I was first married to Iris. I think there is some wonderful chemistry going on between us and I am not willing to just walk away from that. I am going to pursue you until you make up your mind about your damned husband. I'll accept whatever decision you make then, but in the meantime, you and I are going to get to know each other a lot more. I want you to know who I am. I don't want you to go back to that son of a bitch!"

"Could be very dangereuse" She said, pronouncing the word 'dangereuse' with her sexiest French accent. She felt a little bit drunk and relieved that Andrew had not just walked away. They finished their meal, making strangely awkward small talk. After a few minutes, the conversation seemed to lapse and Andrew called for the bill. They stood up to leave and Andrew took one of her hands in his and, looking directly into her eyes, asked.

"Do you still want to stay here tonight?" She responded by putting an arm around him, burying her face on his shoulder, "Yes, I need to get to know you better too"

They found their room on the second floor of the inn. The luxurious hall carpet muffled their footsteps but the old wood floors creaked, betraying their presence. Hollingsworth fumbled with the huge, old fashioned door key and opened the door, letting Nicole pass. He stepped in and closed the door behind him. She turned to him, looking up into his eyes and put both arms around him, kicking off her high heels. He cradled her head in one hand, holding her body close to him with other and kissed her tenderly. Her mouth opened to him she held him close, her hand reaching up into his hair. Then, she suddenly went limp. She seemed to pass out. But she was conscious.

"God! Kiss me again like that please" she whispered.

He picked her up and lay her down on one of the two queen sized beds in the room. He removed her shoes and covered her up with the duvet. She was already asleep. He lay down on the other bed, kicking off his own shoes and turning off the light at the console between the beds. He stared at the ceiling, trying to collect his thoughts. But his thoughts refused to gel and he fell into a fitful sleep.

When he woke up the next morning he was lying on his side in an almost fetal position. She was asleep lying against his back with her knees drawn up under his, and one arm wound tightly around his chest. He could feel the warmth of her body and sensed the soft beat of her heart on his back. He tried to move but she grumbled something under her breath, tightened her grip on him and pressed her face closer into the side of his neck. She began kissing his ear while she unbuttoned the front of his shirt.

She finally let him roll over on his back and come face to face with her. She was completely naked. She started to laugh, kissing him all over his face and then, straddling him, she began to kiss his now bare chest.

They made love in the streaming sunshine until they were both completely spent. Afterward, they lay entwined together in silence studying each other's faces.

They made the short trip back to Nice in the comfortable silence known only to couples in that phase of their relationship where just being together is satisfying enough. Hollingsworth drove. She held his hand when he wasn't shifting gears or needed two hands on the wheel in some of the tight hairpin bends. She watched him drive and admired his zest and confidence enjoying the exhilaration of the speed as much as she did.

On the flight back to Paris, Hollingsworth checked his phone and was surprised to find four messages requesting him to call the home office as soon as possible. Nicole was seated next to him in the cramped economy section, an Air France blanket over her lap.

She leaned on his shoulder. "Bad news?" she asked, sensing his discontent at the email messages.

"The boss wants me to call him ASAP" said Hollingsworth. "I have no idea what it's about but he rarely calls with good news"

"Tant pis pour lui." Nicole whispered snuggling closer to him, holding his arm in hers.

"I can't screw him, Nicole, he's my boss." He replied and bent to kiss her on the forehead.

They dozed fitfully until the plane arrived and a pretty flight attendant called for seat backs and tray tables to be returned to their upright position.

"Let's stop off at the exhibition hall and see how they are doing with the breakdown of the booth. I want to make sure that the simulators are packed properly and that they leave room for my bag."

"D'accord" she replied. "I need to check with Joel and see if we have a distribution count for the Magazine." They took an Uber over to the Exhibition Hall and went their separate ways.

"Call me later." he said to Nicole, giving her an affectionate peck on the cheek.

Henry and the booth team were packing up the equipment in the booth.

"Have you seen this" asked Henry, handing Hollingsworth a magazine. It was a copy of the latest "Defense Electronique" folded open at an article entitled "The future of IFF"

Hollingsworth sat down on one of the stools next to the only table that had not yet been packed away and began to read. The article praised Hollingsworth's "honest appraisal" of the state of the art of defense electronics" and went on to reiterate the needs of the industry that Hollingsworth had outlined in his presentation. A couple of lines in the second paragraph had been highlighted by Henry. It intimated that BAE's products were "lagging" the industry and that "Hollingworth had not divulged any plans for BAE to correct that situation. All of this was absolutely true, but presented in black and white in a leading international magazine, it took on a distinctly pessimistic tone.

Hollingsworth now knew why his boss wanted to talk to him so urgently. His first reaction was to get angry at Nicole for publishing the article. But he realized that Joel had merely written an accurate account of his presentation at the symposium. Henry interrupted his thinking.

"The top brass isn't going like that, even if it is true." Said Henry quietly. "What are you going to do?"

"I guess I'll call him." said Andrew. "Everything in that article is exactly what I said at the symposium and everything I said was absolutely true. Maybe this will wake them all up before it's too late!"

"Maybe" retorted Henry, "but I doubt that the stockholders want to hear that."

"I'd better go back to the hotel and make that call. Can you guys manage without me?"

"No problem." Henry replied, turning back to the work crew who had already started dismantling the empty booth. "Good luck Andrew, knock 'em dead"

Hollingsworth stopped at Nicole's booth to tell her he was going back to the hotel, but she wasn't there. Joel was busy cleaning up the booth and looked up at Hollingsworth.

"Great article!" Andrew said sincerely. "Nicely done"

"Thanks" replied Joel, as Hollingsworth tapped in a call for an Uber ride on his cell phone.

Back in his hotel room, Hollingsworth spent twenty minutes collecting his thoughts before making a phone call that he knew might end his career with BAE.

He finally got through to his boss Ralph Conklin - a short fat man, balding, with an irritating habit of saying "y'know" after nearly every sentence he spoke. Before Hollingsworth could say a word, Cronklin opened fire.

"Andrew! What the fuck do you think you are doing? Our stock price took a three-point hit this morning y'know. You had no authority to publish that article without running it by me or our PA people y'know. What the fuck were you thinking?"

Hollingsworth waited for the barrage to end.

"Well first of Ralph, I didn't publish it, the Defense Electronique magazine published it. They accurately reported what I had said at the symposium. That's their job. You know that what I had to say about the industry was true. You and I have had the conversation several times lately."

"Yes! But you didn't have to blab to the whole damn world how fucked up we are y'know. We have had every sheik in Arabia on the fucking phone this morning asking when we are going to replace the crap we put in their fighters. What do you propose we tell 'em?"

Ralph was getting angrier by the second. Hollingsworth visualized Ralph's face going purple while he pounded his flabby fist on the board room table. He was sure there were other people in the room who wanted to see just how Ralph was going to handle this latest mess.

"Maybe it's time they heard the truth Ralph. Our product is too slow and we are being held to ransom by the only company that makes chips fast enough to do the job. Those are the facts. Tell them that!" Hollingsworth's tone had changed to one of defiance.

"Andrew, the plane will be at Le Bourget tomorrow morning. Make sure you are on it. I need you back here for damage control. The first thing you are gonna do is get that fucking frog magazine to print a retraction." Conklin was now so angry he was frothing at the mouth.

"Look Ralph, that won't happen. They printed EXACTLY what I said at the symposium.
There isn't a single word in that article that isn't a true representation of what I said. They won't print a retraction and if we take them to court, we'll lose. I handed out copies of my presentation, for Christ's sake. They took a video of my

presentation! You can't just deny what I actually said."
Hollingsworth spoke in a level tone, like a lawyer summing up.

"Well fuck that!" Ralph was now screaming into the phone. "In
that case, you better get back here and retract your whole
fucking presentation right now!"

"I won't do that Ralph!" Hollingsworth knew that he had just
crossed the line and Ralph would fire him. "You and I both know
that everything I said was true."

Ralph was silent for several seconds. Hollingsworth could now
hear the voices of a few other people in the room that were
picked up by the speaker-phone. He waited for the inevitable
words from Ralph. Eventually, Ralph managed to muster a calm,
professional voice and announced, as much to the room as to
Hollingsworth.

"OK, if that's your attitude I'll have your termination check
ready when you get here tomorrow. Make sure you are on that
plane, Hollingsworth. You will need to formally hand over all the
restricted material you have and your office keys to the Security
personnel who will accompany you when you enter the
building. Please come directly to the office from the Company
plane. Do not discuss this matter with the other passengers.
Understood?"

Hollingsworth felt strangely elated but hurt, He had given his
best to the company for whom he had worked for nearly three
years, and, now he was being fired for the first time in his
career. When he had been sitting in the hotel room in Paris
considering the offer made to him by Husher, he had worried
about leaving BAE. He didn't want to be disloyal. He didn't want
to leave them at a low point in their history. But now he didn't

care. The company's conservative culture had brought BAE down, despite his efforts to persuade the management to change direction.

Hollingsworth paused a few seconds and responded

"No problem Mr. Conklin, I'll be there tomorrow." He said, immediately dropping the first name informality for the benefit of the others he knew were in the room. He said to himself *"they just fired the only engineer in the Company that can dig them out of this hole they are in. I wonder how THAT will go down in the industry press."* He smiled to himself, put the phone down carefully and went to get a beer from the minibar.

He rummaged through his briefcase and found the agreement that Jack Husher had given him. He sat down in the plush armchair put his feet up on the small desk and began to read the agreement again. More carefully this time.

It took him an hour to reread the contact. He would have to move to San Francisco. He wondered if Nicole would come with him. It surprised him when he realized that she meant so much to him that he might not take the job if she didn't agree to come with him. He thought about her for a long time. He couldn't imagine anything better than being married to her and living a new life in San Francisco. Then he remembered that she was married to a man who had beaten her and yet she still contemplated going back to him. He signed the contract and initialed each page as requested. Then he picked up the phone and called Jack Husher.

Husher's phone went to Voice-Mail. "Jack Husher here; sorry, I can't take your call. Please leave a short message and I'll get back to you. Thanks", and then the familiar beep.

"Jack, this is Andrew, Andrew Hollingsworth. I have had a chance to read your contract and would like to take you up on your very generous offer. Please call me back when you have a moment."

Hollingsworth stared out of the window while he finished his beer. "God, I hope she comes with me" was his only thought.

Hollingsworth knew that Nicole would be up to her neck, working on packing up the booth and getting ready to leave. He texted her a message: "*Dinner tonight? Your room or mine*", followed by a string of heart emoticons.

"*Can't do dinner. Celebrating with the gang and a few advertising clients. U R welcome to come. Cocktails @ 1800 in the Atrium Room.*" Hollingsworth pondered for a moment if he should go but decided he didn't want to be at a party if Jack Husher called him back.

"*That's your show, Nicole. I'll skip it thanks. I need to make some phone calls. Come to my room B334 if you are still upright after the party. I have some news.*" He called the front desk and had some flowers delivered with no card to Ms. Batault in the Atrium Room.

Jack Husher called Hollingworth's room at 6:30.

"Hello Andrew, this is Jack. I'm so glad you have decided to join us. I think we will do some great things. Have you quit your job at BAE yet?" Jack chuckled at the last question.

"No!" replied Hollingsworth "They fired me!"

"You're Kidding! Was it about that article in Defense Electronique?"

"Yes!"

"The dumb bastards just fired the only guy they had that could fix their problems! That wasn't too smart Andrew. But it's good for us."

"Funny, that's what I thought." said Hollingsworth and they both laughed.

"How soon can you be in San Francisco?"

The two men talked at length about getting a work visa, moving, getting a furnished place initially and buying a home later. Finally, Husher said "There's a lot of paperwork needs to be done for your visa and issuing your stock options. I'll get my secretary Alison to contact you and send the stuff you need. If you have any questions or concerns, call me right away, you have my cellphone number".

"I do!" said Andrew, the excitement rising in his voice.

"Great! Welcome aboard Andrew, it's really, really good to have you on the team. I'll see you in a few weeks. Let me know your ETA when you get that settled."

Husher hung up the phone. Hollingsworth held the phone in his hand for several minutes, staring at the mouthpiece. He had a new job in a company in which he would have some significant ownership, a boatload of money, and he was moving to a new country all on the basis of a twenty-minute phone call. Amazing!

He put the phone down and leaped up, punching his clenched fist in the air.

"Yes!" he screamed into the empty room as he strutted over to the minibar and got himself another beer.

Hollingsworth was dozing when Nicole knocked softly on the door. He got up and opened the door. She was standing there with a bottle of champagne in one hand and a dozen roses in the other. She was wearing a stunning red silk dress.

"This is for us," she said holding out the bottle of Champagne. "and these are for me, from a secret admirer."

"Who is he? I'm jealous!" replied Hollingsworth, taking the bottle of champagne.

"I think I know," she said snuggling up to him as she kicked off her high-heels and draped her coat over the chair. "So, what's the big news?"

"I got fired today" Hollingsworth announced, pouring the $100 champagne into two plastic cups. Hollingsworth told her the whole story about the call from Ralph and how he felt quite elated when it was over. Nicole was dumbfounded.

"I can't believe they would do that" she exclaimed. "Merde, Quel Cornichons!"

He went on the tell her about the call to Jack Husher. He hedged around the issue of having to move until, finally, he had to tell her.

"Nicole, I am moving to San Francisco and I want you to come with me. I want you to leave that asshole, permanently and come to the USA with me."

Nicole put down her glass and stood up taking his face in both her hands.

"I am so happy for you Andrew. It's what you have always wanted" She put both arms around him with her face against his chest. She held him so tight he could barely breathe. Her perfume was intoxicating.

"Will you come with me?" he said into her hair.

"This is too much all at once Andrew, I need to digest it all. Let's talk about it later".

With that, she dragged him reluctantly to the bed. They talked endlessly through the night: Andrew declaring his love for her and decrying her husband's violence, Nicole blaming herself for her husband's behavior and a need to give the marriage "another chance".

It didn't make sense to Andrew. If she wanted to give Koudechah another chance, what was she doing in my bed not his?

Nicole was up first, claiming that she had to pack and be ready by 7 am. Hollingsworth ordered breakfast. They didn't talk about San Francisco until she was ready to leave.

"Good luck in San Francisco" she whispered to him as she kissed him goodbye. He could see the tears well up in her eyes and he let her go. He canceled the room service breakfast. He hadn't the stomach for it.

Henry knocked on his door at 9:25.

"Ready?" he said. Hollingsworth checked the room once more for any belongings and found Nicole's scarf under the bed. He put it in his pocket and closed the door behind him.

The plane was waiting on the apron with the engines running.

Gifu, Japan

The Corporate Offices of Subiki Corporation were Spartan to say the least. The floors were polished tile. The windows had aluminum frames like those found in government buildings. The boardroom contained a plain wooden table surrounded by 12 hardwood chairs without cushions. A small table at one end of the room was furnished with a modern coffee maker. The only décor in the windowless room was a Japanese flag at one end of the room. Above the table hung a large portrait of Koji Imakita, the founder of the company.

Imakita had been born in the USA and spent several years in an internment camp in Manzanar, California. His mother and father had died at the camp. He was provided an education in the USA and obtained a master's degree in Business at Stanford University. He renounced his American citizenship as soon as he graduated and moved to Japan to take an entry-level job with Mitsubishi. Koji Imakita spent ten years with Mitsubishi and rose to become the head of aircraft production. He left Mitsubishi to form his own company which was one of the first Japanese companies to use Computer-Aided Design (CAD) technology to manufacture precision parts for aircraft and automobiles.

Imakita's son Keiji, who was born in Gifu, followed in his father's footsteps and took over management of the company when his father passed away. Keiji studied electronic engineering at Ritsumeikan University in Japan, and after graduation had helped design several integrated circuits used in guidance systems.

As electronics had become a larger and larger part of the cost of modern aircraft, Keiji had persuaded his father to diversify into making integrated circuits specifically for the aircraft industry in which the company was already well respected. A new division was formed and headed by Keiji. The division developed a suite of integrated circuits used in guidance, navigation and radar systems, known collectively as "Avionics". Through its connections in the aviation industry, the company soon became a leading manufacturer of these "silicon chips" and sold their products all over the world.

Recently, demand for military avionics had risen sharply in a progressively less stable world. Commercial avionics had also grown as airlines sprouted up in third-world countries and grew at double-digit rates in Asia. All the suppliers of the integrated circuits that went into these devices were short of production capacity.

As a leading producer of these chips, Subiki was faced with the dual problems of how to increase production and how to allocate the limited amount of available product to key customers. Most of Subiki's customers used the chips in Military applications. Who got the products, and who didn't, was becoming a highly volatile international political issue.

A meeting was called to discuss corporate strategy. The Vice President of operations, the Director of Quality Control, and the VP of International sales were already seated at the table when Keiji entered the room with another man. Those seated immediately stood up. Keiji introduced his guest as a consultant. The Japanese director of US sales had flown in from the USA especially for the meeting. The Director of Middle Eastern Sales, Mr. Shibayama, arrived a few minutes late, having encountered delays in his flight from Teheran. He had recently taken over as the Director of the Middle East region. He bowed deeply to

Imakita and the board and apologized profusely for his tardiness.

Imakita stood at the head of the table and spoke authoritatively in Japanese. "Gentlemen, we are facing both a major problem and a major opportunity today. Our new 8706 IFF chip has taken the market by storm. Largely because of the superior speed and reliability of the product we are now the number one supplier. Unfortunately, we can't meet the current demand and this will result in the loss of market share unless we can resolve this problem quickly.

"If we solve this problem we will be presented with a huge opportunity. The Americans are equipping their new aircraft with new faster and more capable IFF systems using our chips. A new start-up in the USA has decided to use our chips. According to their advertising, they could be the next Litton Industries". Imakita smiled wryly and rolled his eyes as he made this comment.

"The British have finally decided to upgrade their obsolete IFF products and plan to use our chips. Collectively this could mean that demand will double in the next year and we already have a six-month backlog that we can't deliver. "To complicate things even further, the Russians just announced that they will supply 75 new Sukhoi 58A fighters to the UIA. They need IFF systems."

Imakita went on to describe the dilemma in which the company now found itself.

"We have a limited supply of chips right now. If we sell these to the Russians it will enable them to equip the fighters they are selling to the UIA with the best IFF systems on the market today. If we do that, we will face a political firestorm from the

USA and could lose that entire market. Israel will be very unhappy, and they build one quarter of all the IFF systems sold worldwide. That would be a big market to lose!"

Imakita took a sip of tea from the porcelain cup on the table in front of him and continued, cup in hand.

"On the other hand, if the UIA hold together the alliance of Arab States that they have created, they will surely upgrade their arms. They could easily become a market far greater than Israel. Missing entry into that market would be disastrous."

He put the cup back down on the table and said "This is a critical decision, so I have asked Mr. Shibayama to spend a few minutes briefing us on the UIA."

"Thank you, sir." Shibayama took to the floor and began to outline the history and current situation in the Middle East. Imakita retrieved his teacup and took a seat at the far end of the table.

"The UIA essentially came about as a result of Hillary Clinton's actions at the time she was Secretary of State. Several of the various insurgent groups consolidated after she failed to nip the insurgency in the bud. Trump's foreign policy has exacerbated the problem. Nixing the nuclear deal incensed the Iranians. They became the catalyst for the UIA the very day that Trump announced that he would cancel the agreement. Moving the American Embassy to Jerusalem, another Trump decision turned the Palestinians toward the UIA. When Trump announced at Davos that he would shut off aid to Palestine unless they seriously talked peace, they were furious.

"Turkey is still reeling from having American funding cut off by Trump. I can understand that. The funding was paying for Turkish soldiers to fight American troops who were assisting anti-Assad insurgents. A really stupid situation.

"Finally, the recent slaughter of the Royal family in Saudi Arabia and, the takeover of the government by Shiite rebels has the world in fear of chaos in the Middle East. It is a foregone conclusion that they will join the UIA.

"Many people, including myself, believe that the American rush to oil independence is driven directly by the unrest in the Middle East and the demise of the Venezuelan oil industry. The USA now has a surplus of oil they are selling to China. That will bankrupt the Saudis"

After a short question and answer period, Shibayama summed up.

"In my opinion, the UIA will succeed over the short run and it will become a substantial market that we should not overlook."

After a break for lunch and a long discussion about how to rapidly increase production capacity, Imakita addressed the board again.

"Gentlemen," he said, there being no women in the room. "I believe we must implement the plan we discussed today to immediately increase our production capacity. We should divert as much as a quarter of our production capacity which is being used for other products to fill this need."

Imakita cleared his throat

"While we bring our capacity into line with the current demand, we will supply all the requirements of the UIA as a first priority. That will ensure our entry into this market."

Shibayama bowed slightly, then interrupted.

"This will put the Americans at a disadvantage, sir"

Imakita looked up at the portrait of his father.

"Yes, I know," and turned to leave the room.

San Francisco

Hollingsworth arrived at San Francisco International in the late afternoon. His special visa status allowed him to breeze through immigration.

"Welcome to the USA" said the cheery Immigration Officer, who was obviously of Asian descent.

"Thank YOU!" responded Hollingsworth as he retrieved his passport and went to get his baggage.

Jack Husher was waiting for him at the exit to Customs.

"Hello Andrew! How was your flight?"

"Long!" replied Hollingsworth

"It's not far into town. I have booked you into a hotel near the office. It's not the 'Four Seasons' but it's nice and has a dining room where you can get breakfast in the morning."

Husher took Hollingsworth's bag and they made their way through the maze of the SFO parking garage. Hollingsworth was surprised that Husher was driving a Nissan Altima. He had expected a big Mercedes. The trunk was a jumble of water toys and kids' clothes, which Husher had to move to make room for the suitcases.

"Grandkids" said Husher; then, as an afterthought,. "We'll lease you a car when you get settled in."

Husher negotiated the traffic out of the airport onto Highway 101 North and began to fill Hollingsworth in with the events of the last few weeks. Husher explained that they had rented office and lab facilities near an area known as South Park, an area that contained several startups and a few larger companies that had survived the dot-com cataclysm at the turn of the millennium.

"Right now, it is just office space for admin and engineering plus about 20,000 square feet of lab space, which is empty. I have hired Gordon Hadley to help get us set up. He was running one of our other companies which we recently sold and he didn't really fit into the corporate culture of the new owners, so he is a free agent right now. He has done several successful startups but gets bored once the growth rate levels off. If you two make a good team he may be the right guy for CEO starting out.

"Accounting will be done by our people until we get things rolling. Same for personnel. But we need a really good person to handle procurement. I have interviewed a couple of People, and so has Gordon, but they were all 'corporate' types not too comfortable in an unstructured situation. Got any ideas?"

"Peter McFarlane is a really good procurement guy but I am not sure you would get him and his wife to move here."

They arrived at the Herbert hotel and Husher got out of the car and retrieved Hollingsworth's baggage.

"I'll pick you up at 10 tomorrow. Get some rest and contact Peter if you have time."

"Ok, see you in the morning" Hollingsworth was feeling the effects of the eight-hour time difference and was beginning to fade mentally.

The next day Hollingsworth arose early and took a continental breakfast in the small hotel lobby. Jack pulled up at the foyer at exactly 10 am. Hollingsworth got in the car and Jack handed him a single sheet of paper. It had the words DO LIST and the date scrawled across the top and about 20 items listed below with names written in a different hand alongside.

"This is our morning brief," said Husher. We meet every morning at 7 am while we are trying to get this show on the road. Everybody does whatever is needed, getting phones, internet, furniture, hiring.   Whatever it takes. We do have an overall plan, but over the years I have found that getting the team together every day creates camaraderie and gets stuff done a lot quick than endless staff and committee meetings.

Once we get the place organized things will change, but for now, everybody mucks in and does whatever is needed. That includes you. I put you down for getting us a good procurement guy and making a list of the lab equipment we already have and what we need. Anything else you want to be involved in, just jump in. Don't be shy. But don't get in the way either. These people will mow you down." Husher looked over and laughed.

It took Hollingsworth 4 days to recover from jet lag and he was glad they had Sunday off so he could sleep in. The place was a whirlwind of activity. The Chief Financial Officer, who picked out colors for carpets and paint and chose furniture. seemed to have no other qualification for that job other than being female.

"It needs a woman's touch" she kept saying when challenged by a male in the team.

The communications guru was a lab technician who had set up a home theatre in his house and was now installing a secure and very fast fiber optic network in the building.

"This way we will have one person on our staff who knows how all this works" said Jack, "we won't have to rely on some snotty kid who has worked at Sisco for two weeks.

One afternoon we all got an app on our cell phones that gave us access to the building and tracked who came in and out and when. The system more than met the security requirements demanded by the US Military of any company that worked on restricted or secret systems. When it was tested, the guru had forgotten to put his phone in the system and had to be let into the building by another employee. That was an occasion for a little celebration.

Hollingsworth called Peter as soon as the secure phones were up and working. He called him at his home in the evening rather than at work.

"Hi Peter, its Andrew. How are things going?" Hollingsworth asked nonchalantly.

"Hi Andrew, it's good to hear from you, I've been meaning to call you. I'll tell you the shit hit the fan at BAE the day you left. We had security people all over the place, and the old man looked like he was about to have a bloody heart attack. The rumor mill said that it was all about that article in Electronic Defense Magazine. I read that, it seemed to me that we all knew that stuff but nobody had published it quite so succinctly up until then. Is that why they let you go?"

"Pretty much" replied Hollingsworth. "Are you still working there?"

"Yes, I am, but it sucks. We can't get the microprocessors and other components we need for the new model you designed, and the Arabs are all over us every day, pressuring us to deliver systems to replace the crap in the fighters we sold them two years ago. Since I'm the purchasing guy, all the crap comes downhill onto my desk."

"What's keeping you there?" asked Hollingsworth.

"That's a bloody good question Andrew. Dianne is about to retire from the airlines and I am tired of this place. It's no fun working for a loser!"

"I'm working for a start up in San Francisco called ERI. We need a guy like you who knows his way around the supply industry. Would you and Dianne move to the USA? You'll make a lot more money and pay half what you are paying in taxes in the UK"

"Are you serious?" asked Peter.

"Yes, never more so"

"What time is the next plane" asked Peter. "What about visas and all that stuff? I hear it isn't easy getting into the US unless you are a Guatemalan refugee." They both laughed.

"I'm serious Peter. Talk to Dianne and see if she is willing to move to San Francisco. You will have to live over here. If you are interested let me know and I'll get the Company to put an offer in the mail to you within a few days. We'll take care of visas and your moving expenses"

"She'll be back from her trip the day after tomorrow. I'll call you." Hollingsworth hung up. He heard Peter say "Holy shit" under his breath as he was putting the phone down.

"Got 'im" thought Hollingsworth as he put the phone down.

Hollingsworth spent the next two weeks taking inventory of the equipment they had in the lab. It included some very expensive radar systems that had been made in Russia. They were obsolete. The Chinese radars were modern and looked like copies of American systems with Chinese characters on the placards. Even the design of the cases was the same. Lots of high-tech equipment was still in its original unopened packaging.

When Hollingsworth asked Husher where he had obtained Chinese systems, he was abruptly told that he didn't need to know.

Several days after Hollingsworth had begun working at the lab, Jack took him aside after the morning briefing was adjourned.

"Houston" Jack said mimicking the infamous Apollo incident, "we have a problem." He showed Hollingsworth a clipping cut from a Japanese Business magazine, with a translation attached. It announced the decision by Subiki Incorporated to cease selling their microprocessors to the USA. It cited various reasons, including the desire to "be fair" to the newly formed Arab alliance, the UIA.

"We need to inform the board about this." Said Husher in a more serious tone, and then spoke aside, to his secretary who sat at a desk outside his spartan office: "Barbara, we need to call a special meeting of the board. Can you send out a formal meeting announcement? Let's try for next Wednesday afternoon. Call each of them on the phone and see if they can make it... you know the drill. We'll need a quorum. Teleconference will work but I'd prefer their physical presence."

Barbara nodded an acknowledgement and Husher led Hollingsworth into his office. The walls of the office were a pale green that had been favored by the previous owners of the building. A single metal desk stood in front of the window. It looked as though it had passed through the Goodwill store several times in its long life. The office chair looked like it had shared the same history. A framed picture of Albert Einstein hung on one wall and several pictures of covered bridges hung on the opposite wall.

Hollingsworth took a seat at one of the five chairs surrounding a small round table in the corner of the office. The chairs looked new. The table, not so much. Husher took two bottles of water from a small refrigerator near the door and sat down opposite Hollingsworth.

"This is deal-breaker Andrew," Husher said quietly, placing the bottles of water on the table. "Without the microprocessors, we don't have a viable business. You know that."

Andrew unscrewed the top on one of the bottles, and after taking a sip of water answered "Of course."

"Any ideas?" asked Husher, making eye contact with Hollingsworth. Despite the obvious seriousness of the situation, Husher seemed completely relaxed, leaning back in his chair with an air of expectancy. He raised his right hand, palm open and fingers spread, inviting a comment from Hollingsworth.

"Of course!" replied Hollingsworth.

Husher smiled a wry smile, his eyes were twinkling again.

"When I did the last design iteration for BAE, I tried to get them to consider using parallel processors. We were already reaching the speed limitations of the current microprocessors and parallel processing was the only way to get a quantum leap in system response speed. But they wouldn't buy it because it was "unproven technology" and would require an entirely different software architecture. That product would be on the market now if BAE had not been so conservative."

Hollingsworth's confident tone inspired Husher to ask "Is that still a viable solution, and where do we get the microprocessors that we need to do it. Doesn't it take more chips to process the data in parallel? Isn't that going make the situation worse?" Husher was now leaning forward in his seat, focused intently on Hollingsworth's every word.

"No problem," explained Hollingsworth. "We may get a tenfold increase in speed using parallel processing, so we can use much slower chips and still obtain a much faster system response than the current serial processing systems using the fastest chips available."

Hollingsworth went on... "Each chip does a small part of the calculation separately. For example, one chip may calculate the distance to the target based on the time it takes for the radar echo to reach the receiver while another chip is verifying the direction of the target using the GPS coordinate data imbedded in the IFF signal. If each of these calculations took one microsecond then a serial system would take two microseconds to complete both calculations whereas the parallel processor would only take one."

"Yes," replied Husher but now we need two chips, not one. The chips are in short supply and now we need twice as many. I don't get it. Where do we get them?"

"Nintendo games!" exclaimed Hollingsworth laughing.

"You are joking of course." Husher's eyes were serious again.

"No!" reassured Hollingsworth. "The Nintendo chips are plenty fast enough and readily available. When Toys-R-Us went belly up a few years ago, thousands of Nintendo games wound up as scrap. I'd bet that some of those are still around in warehouses now. In any case, we could buy brand new Nintendo games off the shelf for less than the price of the Japanese Chips!"

"It's the software development that's the problem. That hasn't ever been done for this application and we really can't estimate what it would cost until we figure out how to "segment" the process into parallel blocks.

"Can you do that by Wednesday?" asked Husher.

"You're joking of course?" retorted Hollingsworth, echoing Husher's earlier comment. A long discussion followed about programming parallel processors. After an hour, Husher finally sat back and declared:

"I think I get it!" I need you to describe this concept in a couple of paragraphs. Add to that your best guess of the time it will take to develop a system and complete the software. Then make your best guess at the performance of the system versus the fastest stuff on the market today. Three pages max, ok?"

"OK" Hollingsworth nodded. "But don't expect too much."

"And see if you can get Peter over here ASAP. Offer him a joining bonus... whatever it takes. We will need to start sourcing these new processors immediately." Husher rose from his chair and opened the door for Hollingsworth to leave.

"Thanks Andrew, all is not lost. We are going to need some more money to do this but I think we can raise that."

The following Wednesday, Husher told the board about the shortage of microprocessors and the need for a change in design strategy. He then presented a five-page request to the Board of Directors for an additional $1,250,000 funding, diluting the ownership of the founders to 33%. The first three pages described a new approach to the design, which was expected to quadruple the response performance of the IFF system at close to the same cost. The fourth page compared the performance of the new system to those currently on the market and forecast the impact of the chip shortage on future sales of those products based on current technology. The last page outlined how the cash would be spent and listed several progress milestones.

By the time Husher finished his presentation, the investors who formed the majority of the board were convinced that the chip shortage was a blessing, since it had forced the corporation to rethink its technical strategy and that they had bet on a sure winner. Funds would be made available in a few days.

Peter accepted the job and arrived in San Francisco a month later. Within a few weeks there were more Nintendo games in the store room than they had at the local Walmart.

Two teenagers from the local High School worked three hours per day after school, carefully extracting the microprocessor chips from the games. The company could have easily purchased the chips from the Japanese manufacturer but Husher had decided that "discretion was in order". The Chinese industrial spies who had infiltrated every corner of Silicon Valley, were unlikely to notice that the employees were buying Nintendo games. Hollingsworth virtually lived at the lab for the next 3 months. The three programmers he hired seemed to live the same way. They lived on McDonald's breakfast muffins and Thai or Chinese take-out.

Anne-Marie, the fiery red-headed girlfriend of one of the programmers burst into the lab one night screaming at her boyfriend

"It's time to go home John! It's me or this shit-hole. Make up your mind!" John barely looked up. The other two continued with their work as if in some kind of a trance.

"I can't go home 'til he goes home!" said John. "We have work to do. How did you get in here anyway?" He finally looked up at her.

"He doesn't have a fucking home to go to John. You do!" Anne-Marie spat back and strode out.

"Go home John" said Hollingsworth "all of you go home"

A week later, Anne-Marie re-appeared at the lab at 6 p.m. The programmers were all in their usual trance. Hollingsworth greeted her gruffly.

"You really are going to have to tell us how you get in here ,Anne-Marie." She ignored him.

"Come with me!" she said

She led him out of the back door of the building where the trash containers were kept.

"They never lock this door" she said. "This is where the employees come out for smoke Breaks or whatever"

They meandered through the streets and avenues for twenty minutes, Anne-Marie now dragging him reluctantly by the cuff of his jacket. Now in a gentrified residential area, they entered a two-story Edwardian apartment building typical of that area of San Francisco. She led him in silence to a second-floor apartment and opened the door.

"What's this all about" asked Hollingsworth, now slightly out of breath.

The two-bedroom apartment was warm and cozy. Furnished in typical "early Good Will" stuffed chairs, a few antiques from the 1950's and a bed with a head-board and a very British looking floral bedspread.

"This is yours! Get a fucking life Andrew so I can get my boyfriend back. OK?" Then she left him to find his own way back.

Peter appeared at the door of the apartment.

"Nice" he said.

"Did you put them up to this Peter? This is mutiny on the Bounty you know."

Peter went into the tiny kitchen a got a couple of beers from the fridge. They both sank into the stuffed armchairs.

"You were burning them out Andrew. Anne-Marie came to me for help. Jack and I agreed, you can't run this program for ever on afterburners. These people worship you, Andrew. They will work until they drop dead if you let them. Besides, you really do need a life. How long is it since you talked to Nicole?"

Hollingsworth took a long draught from the bottle of beer.

"You're right of course. But we are getting so close! The hardware all works now and most of the software works on its own. We just can't make the integration work reliably,"

Andrew went on excitedly about the huge progress they had made with the new system. Peter interrupted his stream of consciousness,

"How long is it since you talked to Nicole Andrew?"

"I dunno" replied Andrew, draining his beer, "C'mon. Let's get back to work."

Everybody had gone home when they got back to the lab.

"Let's go get your stuff from the hotel and I'll take you home, I doubt if you could find the place on your own, and you have too much crap to carry,"

Work at the lab seemed to be just as intense after the "Anne-Marie Intervention", as it became known. They hired a fourth programmer who had more experience with parallel processors and they had a new rule that they all had to go home for dinner.

Fewer mistakes were made because the programmers weren't mentally exhausted. The weekly progress meetings started to reflect more and better teamwork. Finally, six months, to the day after they had moved into the building. One quiet voice in the corner said,

"Shit! it's all working Sweep me again!"

The entire team huddled around the programmer's desk while the RADAR simulator at the other end of the lab "swept" the virtual reality airspace and pinged the aircraft. The system immediately identified the source of the Radar signal and transmitted a fake "Friend" response. The process took about a quarter of the time the BAE system took to respond to the same signal, Hollingsworth was ecstatic and screamed "Eureka!", shaking hands with every member of the team who were gathered now in the corner of the lab.

They had a new product but now it had to be tested in the real environment in which it would be used. They had to sell it to the US Military.

"When can I get 10 working prototypes?" asked Hollingsworth. "You guys figure the best and worst case and send me an email. Then GO HOME!

Two days later, Jack Husher sent a secure e-mail to his contact in the US Airforce:

> To General Roger D. Hall:
> Re: project Epsilon we discussed in DC
>
> >The new software is now working.
> >The product is at least three times faster than anything on the market today.
> >It uses readily available components.
> >I'll have 50 prototypes ready to test by the 21 of next month.
> >I propose that Ground and Airborne testing is conducted in parallel, advise earliest date we can meet with your team regarding testing location and schedule.
> >Am sending a draft proposal and compliant contract for this activity via the usual secure channels.
>
> Warm Regards
> Jack

A month later, Husher was summoned to a high-level meeting at the Department of Defense located in the Pentagon. The Secretary herself was present, as was General Roger Hall, chief of staff for the US Airforce. A civilian from Israel was present but never identified.

The tension in the room was palpable. There had obviously been some heated discussion before Husher joined the meeting. The Secretary welcomed Husher gracefully and said

"Let me fill you in, Jack"

She informed him of the latest Israeli intelligence, which clearly indicated that the UIA were planning and all-out invasion of Israel. The plan was to knock out Israeli Air Defenses followed by an attack on ground defenses, giving the UIA Air Forces complete air superiority, A "scorched earth" ground attack would follow on all of Israel's borders simultaneously.

The Arabs assumed that, as Trump approached the end of his second term, Congress wouldn't risk entering a war on the side of the Jews, who were unpopular with the indoctrinated US youth. Without US military help, Israel was doomed. General Hall confirmed that the Arab aircraft, now equipped with superior IFF systems, would prevail over the US Aircraft currently operated by Israel.

"My God!" Exclaimed Husher, "I knew the Arabs had been rattling their sabers lately but I had no idea that they were on the verge of a full-scale invasion."

The Secretary smiled.

"That's why I asked you along Jack. I understand from the Pentagon technical gurus that your new electronic gadget will level the playing field for the Israeli Airforce. Is that true?

Husher hesitated for moment, carefully formulating his answer.

"Potentially, yes." Husher replied. "But it's untested. We have no idea how it will hold up in a combat environment...."

The Secretary interrupted him

"I know, and it will take months for us to test it and get it approved by the Pentagon. Even then, Congress could prevent you from selling the product to the Israelis. So..." she went on. "the Israeli government has agreed to test it for us. They will act simply as a sub-contractor for you, which shouldn't have any political implications so long as Congress doesn't quite understand why we are doing this." She smiled again.

"Revise the contract you sent to us. Reframe it as a contract between an Israeli private corporation and your own company. Your Company owns any patents. We happen to have a representative of that company here today" she beckoned to the still unidentified civilian in the room. "He will give you the details. Work out the finances with him. Whatever it takes!"

The Secretary turned to leave the room.

"Thank you, gentlemen." Then, over her Shoulder, she added. "Keep me posted, Roger." and closed the door behind her.

The unidentified civilian came over and introduced himself to Husher. Joseph Ahrens, a well-respected Israeli arms dealer. He sold Israeli weapons all over the world. Roger Hall came over and shook his hand.

"Call me if you need anything. Meanwhile I will arrange transportation to Israel for your guy, Hollingsworth is it. We won't use the airlines, no need to attract the attention of the media at this stage."

They shook hands again and Hall gave him his business card.

"I'll be in touch"

A week later, Husher called Hollingsworth in the evening at home. That was unusual, so Hollingsworth was curious. Husher had briefed him on the deal with the Israelis. He was excited about testing the new product.

"Hi Andrew. Are you alone?"

"Yes"

"Be at Beale Airforce base RECEIVING Gate at 10:30 am Thursday, That's the day after tomorrow, No more than 25lbs of soft baggage. No ID other than passport. Personal belongings only. Absolutely no Company Stuff. None. Nada. Not even your laptop. Got it. Ask for Captain Rojas."

"Sounds a bit 'cloak and dagger' to me but OK. Where am I going?

"I think you know. I am being cautious Andrew. This has to be kept under wraps, even from our own people. I'll talk to you when you get there OK"

"OK." but Husher had already hung up.

Hollingsworth sat down, contemplating the short conversation with his boss. He had helped write the contract with the Israeli Corporation. It was a private company. He wondered why the Airforce was even involved. Strange, he thought but Jack always thinks way "outside the box"

He arrived at Beale on time but some difficulty finding the "Cargo Gate". Captain Rojas was waiting for him. He got into the passenger seat of Hollingsworth's car and directed him to a parking area behind some hangers. They entered the hanger through the small personnel door at the rear of the hangar.

Inside was parked a huge Black Aircraft that looked like something out of a Sci-Fi movie.

"That's an SR72" gasped Hollingsworth, like an excited schoolboy.

"Yes, indeed it is. The successor to the SR71. This is your ride today. Lt. Col Vandervort here will be driving. But first we have to get you prepared. We have a suit for you and you will have to pre-breathe our special Oxygen Cocktail for an hour before you take off. Lt. Col Vandervort will explain."

Rojas shook his hand.

"Even I don't know where you going, sir, but it must be very important to the US Air Force. You're the first civilian to fly in an SR72. Good luck, sir. Enjoy the flight"

Nobody had addressed Hollingsworth by his name.

Four Hours later, the SR72 arrived at Mashabim Airforce base in Israel. Hollingsworth could barely absorb the experience of the flight of nearly 7500 miles at 3000 mph, at altitudes the pilot would not divulge. They had been on the very edge of space, traveling at four times the speed of sound.

Mashabim Air Base, Israel

As soon as the SR72 landed it was surrounded by several heavily armed security vehicles and a large white truck that looked like an ambulance on steroids.

The pilot announced over the intercom: "Here comes our ride. Please keep your visor down. This place is surrounded by people with cameras with telephoto lenses taking pictures of everything that moves."

"OK." Hollingsworth responded. "What's the drill?"

"Just sit tight. They'll bring the bus alongside and station the fire-suppression units alongside. In case you hadn't noticed, the outside skin is still hot enough to fry an egg, and, as we cool down we'll start leaking fuel again like we were in the hangar before we took off. Don't worry - this is all normal and if it does light up it will be quick. You won't feel a thing... so they tell me"

"That's nice to know," Hollingsworth said lightheartedly.

The pilot had not been very talkative during the flight. Hollingsworth imagined he was pretty busy staying ahead an airplane that was moving faster than a high velocity bullet. The conversation had been limited to the pilot pointing out the bigger land marks visible from the edge of space: The Great Lakes, Hudson Bay, Iceland, Greenland, Ireland, all going under them at an incredible rate. Now he was relaxed.

"When the bus get here, I'll open the canopy and they will deploy the egress system. Remember how heavy these suits are, so make sure you are holding on to the railings at all times.

The crew will help you up. Keep your visor down until we are inside the building, OK?"

"Got it!" I replied. "Where are we" Hollingsworth finally asked"

Vandervort laughed, suddenly realizing that he hadn't told his passenger where they were headed. He hadn't known himself until they were airborne, and had no idea who his passenger was.

"We are at Mashabim Airforce base. Welcome to Israel."

Inside the building, the crew helped them to shed their complicated life-supporting space Suits, which protected them from heat inside the aircraft and provided them with a breathable atmosphere where, basically, there was none.

One of the crew checked his blood pressure and oxygen saturation.

"Any nausea, sir" he asked.

"No, I feel fine, thanks," Hollingsworth replied

"Great. Colonel Koudechah will be here shortly" explained the orderly, then left Hollingsworth alone in the room.

A few minutes later, a tall man wearing an Israeli Airforce uniform entered the room. He wore two rows of ribbons above the right breast pocket. Hollingsworth immediately recognized one of them as the Distinguished Flying Cross. The Name tag read simply

Col. KOUDECHAH

He reached out to shake Hollingsworth's hand.

"Welcome to Israel Professor Hollingsworth! We very, very happy that you come help us".

The Colonel's English was stilted and he had difficulty pronouncing Hollingsworth's name in his thick accent, but Hollingsworth got the message. He wanted to tell the Colonel that he wasn't a professor, but decided that could wait.

"Very pleased to meet you" he replied, shaking the Colonel's hand vigorously.

Koudechah put a hand on Hollingsworth's shoulder and directed him to the door at the opposite end of the room.

"Please follow me. We go to meet Minister Gibli. He very important man. I take you in my automobile now. OK Prof?"

"OK Colonel" Hollingsworth responded, smiling; and from that moment onward they addressed each other as "Prof" and "Colonel".

They left the building and got into a bright red Alfa Romeo.

"We meet Mister Gibli at Airforce Administration office. I am official title Assistant Secretary of the Airforce." He pointed at himself, turning to look at Hollingsworth while hurtling down the narrow road at 100 kph. "I am also Janitor" he added, laughing out loud.

After a thirty minute "white knuckle" ride they arrived at an austere building set off from a security fence surrounding what appeared to be another air base. It was guarded by armed Israeli soldiers.

"OK prof! We here."

The guards saluted the Colonel as they entered the building, and one of them held the door open for them.

Inside the building, more soldiers staffed a sophisticated security system with walk-through metal detectors, facial recognition cameras everywhere, and a device that seemed to emit a strange light when anybody walked past it. The soldiers came to crisp attention and saluted the Colonel as he entered.

The Colonel gave a few quiet orders to the Staff Sargent at the desk, and a few minutes later a plastic ID badge on a lanyard was politely handed to Hollingsworth. Koudechah turned to Hollingsworth and said in his broken English, "Even the fucking mice can't get in here without badge!" and they both laughed.

They wound their way through a maze of corridors until they came to an office at the end of the corridor. The white wall next to the double doors was emblazoned with blue plastic letters declaring the occupant to be "The Secretary of the Airforce." In English and Arabic.

"This my office" said the Colonel opening the door for Hollingsworth

A middle-aged man rose up to meet them as they entered the room. The Colonel introduced him as the Minister of Defense, Mr.Gibli.

Gibli reached out his hand to Hollingsworth "Welcome to Israel Mr. Hollingsworth. I cannot tell you how grateful we are that you were willing to come here at short notice. I am sure you're aware that we don't have a lot of time." His English was perfect, with a hint of an American accent. He had a degree from Stanford University in California.

Gibli motioned Hollingsworth to sit down and began to explain the situation in the Middle East. He showed Hollingsworth recent satellite pictures of Arab troops amassed at the Syrian, Lebanese, and Egyptian borders. The Arabs were preparing to drive the Jews into the sea. Jordan and Iraq had fewer forces but it was clear from the satellite photographs that their preparations were underway too. Gibli continued in a serious tone:

"From the intelligence we have gathered, the Arabs plan on attacking our Radar Systems and Ground Defenses and believe that their Aircraft are superior and the we will not be able to stop them. At present, that assumption is true. Their aircraft are in many cases as good as ours, they are the same type of aircraft. They also have the new Russian S27 stealth fighters. But they have superior Electronic Defense systems. The Equipment supplied to Saudi Arabia by the Americans before the invasion by the UIA is, in fact, far superior to ours, except for our F35's. But we only just commissioned those and the pilots aren't trained. We are at a disadvantage and there is little doubt that the Arabs would be able to wipe out most of our ground defenses. After that, they would take out our Air Defenses and, with complete Air Superiority, they would launch the ground attack. It will be a blood bath, and they will win any ground battle because they outnumber us. I cannot contemplate what would happen next"

"Jesus," exclaimed Hollingsworth almost involuntarily
"I don't think he can help us, Mr. Hollingsworth." Gibli
responded in the same serious tone.

An attractive young woman brought in refreshments and left
quickly, obviously aware of the lack of levity in the discussion.
Gibli sat down and poured himself some coffee.

"There is some good new Andrew. May I call you Andrew?" Gibli
didn't invite Hollingsworth to call him by his first name and
didn't wait for Hollingsworth's response.

"First, I am told that your new system will provide our aircraft
with the ability to fire first." That alone will provide us with
superiority, even over faster aircraft. Second," he hesitated,
while he took another sip of coffee and nonchalantly nibbled on
a biscuit, "second, I believe our Electronic Defense gurus have
found a way to hack into the Arab's Satellite system. That will
allow us to identify our fighters as "friendly" to both the enemy
and our own forces."

"You are kidding!" gasped Hollingsworth "How?"

Gibli laughed. His eyes twinkling. "I have no idea, it's all Yiddish
to me. But we have to find a way to integrate that software into
your system. You will have full access to the two kids who
figured it all out."

"Kids?" Hollingsworth repeated.

"Yes, you know the type. They look like they are 14 years old
and haven't bathed or had a haircut in 6 months. I am sure you
employ a few of them yourself."

"I do" said Hollingsworth

Gibli stood up again and looking first at Col. Koudechah and then at Hollingsworth he said. "The future of Israel and the Middle East is in your hands, gentlemen. We don't have any time to waste. Integrate the hacking software as quickly as possible and install the systems in the fleet. We don't have time to test it in the field. Test in battle. We will launch a pre-emptive strike on their defenses as soon as you tell me you are ready."

Hollingsworth and Koudechah looked at each other in astonishment.

"He's right," Said Koudechah. "We have nothing to lose!", and opened the door to leave.

Hollingsworth looked back to see Gibli back at his desk with the phone in his hand.

"Good Luck!" he said, dismissing them with a wave of the phone.

The two men began work immediately. Hollingsworth worked with the two "pimply-kids-in-need-of-baths" to get the software integrated into the prototypes. The software worked by "listening" to the enemy's signals as it queried the satellite system prior to take-off, much like the BAE systems. After logging on, it downloaded the list of friendly codes for the day. The next available code was assigned to the aircraft making the query. Codes didn't have to be entered manually, so fewer errors were made. All that was needed was to log onto the secure satellite system. The Israelis had broken into just about every secure Military Defense system in the world. Finding a way into the relatively unsophisticated system developed very quickly and recently by the UIA wasn't difficult.

Hollingsworth enjoyed working with pimply kids, who started to wear lab coats in order to jokingly elevate their status on the team. They were naïve but open minded, and tackled every problem with a can-do attitude and the energy that only a 24-year-old can muster. Within three days they had one of the prototypes set up. When they turned it on, it displayed a flashing message indicating that it was contacting the Satellite. It took nearly 10 minutes to gain access, but eventually the message changed to "READY"

They couldn't test the system on a real satellite, but the kids were of the opinion that the simulator provided by the US Airforce was "pretty good". The eldest, and most experienced, explained nonchalantly, "you seen one satellite, you seen 'em all. Don't worry, it will work!"

Meanwhile, Col. Koudechah had been working on the problems of mounting the system in the F16 and connecting it up to the existing GPS, Radar systems and Flight Displays on board the aircraft. He called to let him know they had a working system and asked how he was progressing with the physical installation.

"Too many fucking wires!" Koudechah responded to his question, obviously frustrated. "Where there is place to mount, it is either too fucking hot or too far away for fucking wires to plug," Koudechah's knowledge and use of Anglo Saxon was expanding, thought Hollingsworth

"I'll be right over" Hollingsworth said, nodding to his young assistants. "You guys can go! Many thanks for your hard work today."

He walked over to the hangar housing the older F!6D two-seat trainer. It was nearly 8 p.m. Koudechah was wearing a pair of coveralls lying on his back under the belly of the plane. Several inspection covers had been removed, the covers and dozens of screws lay on the floor beside him. Two airframe technicians stood nearby.

Hollingsworth stood over Koudechah and yelled over the sound of nearby air compressor,

"Come on Colonel. Call it a day. I am starving! I haven't eaten since breakfast."

Koudechah slithered out from under the plane and looked at his watch.

"God, it is twenty hundred hours already. I need to call home. There is a little place around the corner where we can eat. I'll buy you a beer." Koudechah spoke on the phone in Hebrew for few minutes while he wriggled out of his coveralls.

"Ciao," he said casually into the phone. "OK Prof," he said, "let's go!"

He turned to the technicians as they left and said in Hebrew, "Don't bother to put the panels back. We will be back on this again early in the morning. Make sure the place is secure. Thanks!"

Hollingsworth was relieved to find that the restaurant they arrived at was Italian. He wasn't keen on kosher food. He realized for the first time that Koudechah wasn't Jewish. He had assumed that, since he was Israeli, he was Jewish. He had the nose.

They got a table and began immediately to talk about the various options they had to mount the system. The mount had to be strong since the aircraft could pull nine G's. The Nintendo chips were designed to work at normal temperatures, so the systems couldn't be mounted anywhere near the engine. They worked out all the possibilities together as they ate and drank a few glasses of red wine.

Gradually they relaxed and began telling stories about their flying experiences. Koudechah had a lot of combat experience and was a qualified F16 test pilot. Israel had over 100 F16's and 75 F35's. Koudechah was also the chief F35 flight instructor. Hollingsworth, whose experience was primarily gliders and single-engine airplanes, was fascinated by some of Koudechah's tales. He couldn't imagine ejecting from a burning jet at 800 kilometers an hour. Koudechah was dumfounded at the idea of flying an airplane a distance of 1500 Km without an engine.

The late dinner became a habit as the two men worked together under intense pressure. They argued, they laughed, and sometimes shared their despair when things didn't work out. The F16 and the IFF system consumed their lives for over ten days. Gibli called Koudechah every day for an update on progress. Every day he told Koudechah the it might only be hours before the Arabs attacked. They started testing the system on the ground. Koudechah sat in the front (Pilot Seat) and Hollingsworth sat in the back. His task was to establish the routine to set up the system and operate it in flight. The F16 is a single seat fighter. Hollingsworth would have to train all the Israeli F16 pilots how to use the system.

On Sunday morning they both arrived at the hanger at 5:30 am. "O' Dark 30"

Koudechah was wearing a flight suit and carried a huge duffel bag from which he pulled a second suit and two G-suits.

"You're expecting me to fly with you?" Hollingsworth asked incredulous. The guy in the back seat was usually a flight instructor or a weapons officer.

"Yes! Who else? You can fly plane. You fly F16 simulator yes, and you know IFF system best! This is 3D simulator LOL. No worries, I guide plane, you make IFF working, OK?"

The ground crew helped them get in the plane. The cockpit was barely large enough. Similar in many ways to his own glider. But he normally wore shorts and a T-shirt in the glider, not a G-suit and a helmet with an integrated oxygen system. Hollingsworth was hot and very nervous. He had flown an F16 simulator many times but this was different. This was for real!

"OK prof?" asked Koudechah over the intercom in the helmet.

"Yes, I think so, I assume the Oxygen is automatic?"

"Yes! We just fly around while you get happy in back. Then you take controls. Stick and rudder only. Then I fly, you turn on systems, OK?"

They were taxiing out as Koudechah was speaking. Hollingsworth heard the pilot talking in Hebrew to the military control tower. Koudechah lined the plane up said over the intercom n the runway and opened the throttle. Hollingsworth was pinned in the seat for several minutes. In five minutes, they were at 7000 meters (24,000 ft), and Koudechah eased the throttle back.

"Your airplane! Don't break it" Koudechah

Hollingsworth took the controls and acknowledged: "My Airplane."

The plane was very responsive, more so than the simulator. But the G-forces aren't apparent in the simulator. He banked over at 45 degrees and did a few simple maneuvers. He felt the G-suit tighten up on his body as the aircraft approached 3 Gs. It was as easy to fly as the simulator, once he had become used to the speed.

"OK. My airplane," said Koudechah after about 15 minutes, "Let's try IFF system"

"Your Airplane" replied Hollingsworth and flipped on the master switch on the IFF panel. The panel lit up and started flashing just as it had in the lab. They waited for what seemed forever, and nothing happened. He tried again. Nothing.

"Is the RADAR system armed?" asked Hollingsworth

"It is now." Answered Koudechah sheepishly.

A few minutes later, the IFF screen began to flash "READY"

"Bingo!" Hollingsworth yelled into the mic.

"We have to get on the ground to verify that it logged onto the satellite!"

Koudechah immediately pulled a 4G Victory roll and hit the afterburners. They were back at the base in twenty minutes. Hollingsworth didn't notice that they broke the sound barrier, he was busy watching an El Al 737 going into Tel Aviv and happy to note the IFF indicated "FRIEND" for that Radar target. The dot on his radar screen went green too. That indicated the IFF system was "talking" to the aircraft RADAR system.

When they landed, Gibli was waiting on the apron for them. He was visibly agitated. As soon the hydraulic cockpit canopy opened, Gibli asked Koudechah (in Hebrew) how the test had gone. Koudechah answered in English, gesturing toward the rear seat with his thumb.

"Ask him, I was flying airplane."

Hollingsworth responded enthusiastically,

"This was a pretty superficial initial test, but nothing fell off and nothing burned. The Satellite hack worked perfectly. We did see a 737 and it showed up as friendly, so that part works. We didn't engage any hostile aircraft so we don't really know whether we look friendly to them of not. What are the Arabs up to?"

The ground crew were close-by, assisting them out of the aircraft. Gibli raised his hand gesturing that they should continue the conversation inside. On the way to the Operations room, Gibli made small talk.

"How did you like flying the real F16? Col. Koudechah told me you had flown the simulator quite a lot."

"It's a fantastic airplane!" exuded Hollingsworth opening the door to the building for Gibli.

Once inside the building and behind the closed doors of the Operations Room, Gibli waited until the two men had removed their flight gear and settled down, each with a bottled soft drink from the vending machine inside the room. The small talk was over.

"We have 5 days Gentlemen. Just 5 days!" Gibli announced again, in a tone a doctor reserves to tell a patient he has terminal cancer, "We have to strike in the next three or four days."

"Fuck!" said Koudechah, adopting his new-found Anglo-Saxon language. "Are you sure?"

Gibli didn't bother to answer. He got himself a soft drink and locked the door. The three men sat at around a small dining table and discussed their options for over an hour. When they finally agreed on a plan, Gibli placed both hands flat on the table and reiterated their decision, slowly and deliberately.

"Colonel, you fly an F16 over the Syrian border tonight. If they think you are friendly, and don't launch an attack or recon, we know the system works. Otherwise you run back over the border and eject if they fire on you and you can't evade. You eject and parachute into Israeli territory. It's imperative that you do not risk being shot down in Syria and captured. Is that clear? No heroics!"

The Colonel nodded and Gibli continued,

"If the system works, we ready the twenty-five F35's for which we have trained pilots and ground test the 50 F16':s that should all be equipped with the new system by the end of the day today. You will have to train those 50 pilots early tomorrow Andrew. Can you do that.?"

Hollingsworth nodded. "Yes" and Gibli continued,

"No matter what happens, we launch AWACS and attack with the F35's at 0400 the next day. The objective is to take out as many of their aircraft on the ground as possible. The F35's will be divided into groups of three. Each group will attack a different base at precisely the same time so the Arabs have no opportunity to warn their brethren. They are to return immediately to refuel and re-arm at the 4 bases we have designated. Those kids don't have the training or the experience to linger for a dog fight. They get in and get back. Understood?" Gibli didn't wait for a response, he continued,

"If the system works correctly, we launch the F16's and attack their Ground Defense Radars and their airborne support systems on the ground with twenty planes. The rest should be armed with anti-tank and anti-personnel weapons and will attack the ground forces. Again, this must occur on ALL fronts starting at precisely 04:00. We won't talk about what happens is the system doesn't work. The F16's will be launched anyway but they will be no match for any of the surviving Arab fighters and they will be vulnerable to ground-to-air missiles. It will be a blood bath." Gibli stood up

"Have we covered everything Gentlemen?"

Both men nodded agreement and headed back to the Operations room.

"What time are we leaving for Syria" asked Hollingsworth. Koudechah stopped walking and turned to Hollingsworth

"No need for you coming, Professor. Too much risky. You show me how work system they install in single seat F16's. I not flying trainer into Syria." Koudechah's tone was stern.

"I'm coming with you Colonel, if I have to fly that thing myself!" They stood in silence for some time, trying to stare each other down. Finally, Koudechah caved and said "Ok, if you're serious, have the lieutenant show you how to operate the Ejector seat. We will take off an hour after sunset." With that, Koudechah ordered the ground crew to refuel the trainer and strode off.

Hollingsworth worked all day, preparing a simple set of written instructions and a check-list for the pilots who would be using the system for the first time. They wouldn't have time to read instructions in combat. They only had to learn how to arm the system prior to takeoff , understand what the indicators on the panel meant when they came on in flight, and how to interpret the various messages. It wasn't rocket science, but it was.

He met with the Lieutenant and was briefed on the use of the Martin Baker Ejector Seat. That wasn't rocket science either, but it really was. Hollingsworth was nervous about being fired out of the aircraft on top of a rocket propelled seat accelerating at nearly 10G. He prayed he wouldn't have to use it.

He met Koudechah outside the operations room as the sun was disappearing below the horizon. The weather was perfect. Koudechah came up to him and said quietly

"No need for you coming Professor, you sure you want to be coming?"

"Yes" Hollingsworth replied immediately, getting into his flight gear. They took off 45 minutes later, heading out over the Mediterranean Sea. Koudechah lit the afterburners and Hollingsworth watched the Mach indicator go past 1.0 and climb to Mach 1·40, about 1100 miles per hour. In less than an hour Koudechah made a right turn and leveled the plane out at 22,000 ft. They flew toward the coast, and within minutes were over land, flying parallel to the Syrian border about five miles inside Syrian territory.

Hollingsworth could see what looked like tanks and troop carriers gathered along some of the roads. His mouth was dry and he found himself sweating a little. Every few seconds the red LED on the front of the IFF panel would flash, indicating a RADAR contact.

"Radar contact" Hollingsworth announced over the intercom.

After 10 minutes, Koudechah turned 180 degrees and headed back out to sea paralleling the border a little further into Syrian territory. Hollingsworth could hear the Colonel's shallow breathing over the intercom and thought to himself, "he's as scared as I am"

Nothing happened!

Koudechah continued out to sea beyond Syrian radar range and descended to 1000 feet above the water.

"Looks like it works, Professor. Wanna fly it home?" he asked Hollingsworth, who found he had stopped sweating but was still shaking.

"Love to! My airplane Colonel." They both laughed, and the shaking stopped.

They got back to the base on schedule and Koudechah executed a perfect barrel roll down the runway with full afterburners.

"If we awake," Koudechah spoke into the intercom, "they awake too.", laughing out loud into the mic.

By the time they landed and got into the building, half the operational staff was in the ops room in various stages of dress. They cheered as the two pilots entered the room.

"I gather it worked" Gibli said sternly, obviously not happy with the noisy fly-by.

The next day the base was a flurry of activity, with aircraft being fueled and armed, and groups of pilots getting briefed on their individual targets. It seemed like hundreds of new people had appeared on the base from nowhere. Gibli had gone back to Tel Aviv. Koudechah was working with the new F35 pilots. He was like a mother hen with new chicks.

Hollingsworth was having lunch with a couple of the F16 pilots he had been briefing about the IFF system when Koudechah came over to the table. The pilots all stood and saluted the Colonel who motioned them to be seated.

"Prof, "Koudechah said, interrupting the conversation. "You invited at my home for dinner tonight," he said clumsily. "Meet wife and have drinks. We launch early next morning so last chance to thank you for so much all you do for Israel. I pick you up at hotel at 16:30, we drive to Tel Aviv"

"Ok, great. That will be nice!" But Koudechah was already striding out of the room before Hollingsworth could finish the sentence.

"I've never seen the old man that nervous," said one of the pilots, as the group broke up. Hollingsworth decided to go back to the hotel, take a nap and freshen up. It had been a grueling few days.

That evening, Koudechah picked up Hollingsworth in the red Alfa. Koudechah didn't talk much - instead, focusing his attention on pushing the car to its limits. Hollingsworth found himself using the brakes he wished he had on his side of the car as they rocketed toward what seemed to be one impossible corner after another. They arrived in Tel Aviv with Hollingsworth concluding that the flight over the Syrian border had been safer, but for some reason, he wasn't shaking.

They parked in the courtyard below Koudechah's home and Koudechah led the way to the townhouse. He was fumbling with the keys to the heavy wooden front door when it was opened by his wife. Hollingsworth was dumbfounded and felt the blood drain from his head. Standing in the doorway was the woman he knew as Nicole Batault, the editor of Defense Eleqtronique magazine, looking as beautiful as he remembered her, one year ago.

"Professor, I like you meet my wife, Nicole."

Hollingsworth couldn't find words. A jumble of thoughts flashed through his mind. The first was that he loved this woman dearly. A woman who had gone back to her husband after he left her with little option in Paris. A husband who had beaten her cruelly on several occasions, he suspected. A man he had worked with for nearly six months and come to admire. A man with whom he had risked his life. It was impossible to mentally digest it all!

His mind went into the survival mode he had learned as a pilot. When everything turns to crap, just fly the plane, just fly the plane, aviate, navigate then communicate. Hollingsworth's mind went on autopilot.

"We've met" said Hollingsworth calmly "We met at the Paris Air Show, I believe. I was in the booth next to you." He extended his hand to her in greeting. "Nice to see you again!"

Nicole had gone pale with shock, but smiled gracefully. Their eyes met briefly. A plea for discretion by her, and instant accord by him, was exchanged without words. The color returned to Nicole's cheeks. She was safe. She knew instinctively that none of the past would be revealed. If Michel ever found out what had happened in Paris, he would kill her. She was certain of that now.

Dinner conversation started with awkward small-talk. Michel drank most of the first bottle of red wine and all of the second. He dominated the conversation after dinner, describing the plan for tomorrow's attack on the Arabs. He was obviously relishing the carnage he expected Israel to inflict on the unwitting Arabs, thanks to Hollingsworth's "magic box". Nicole interrupted his tedious tirade by serving brandy in the living room. Michel soon fell asleep.

Nicole went into the lobby to get Hollingsworth coat and came back into the living room. Her eyes were flooded with tears.

"I'll drive you back to your hotel," she said gently, proffering the coat. "Let's go!"

She bent over Michel and told him loudly in Hebrew that she was going to take Andrew back to his hotel. He grunted something about the Alfa and went back to sleep. Hollingsworth wondered what kind of shape he would be in for combat the next morning.

Nicole locked the big wooden door and they made their way to the car in silence. It wasn't until they were out of the courtyard on the street that Andrew asked "Why? Nicole, why did you go back to that brute?"

"You went off to San Francisco and I needed to give my marriage a second chance. I told you that. You have been working with Michel for months now. You must know that he is a really great person. He's only a brute when he gets drunk and belligerent."

"Has he ever hit you again?" Hollingsworth asked in a stern tone.

"No" she replied quickly.

"But you know he would kill both of us if he ever found out about what happened in Paris, don't you?"

"Yes" she replied, "he probably would." Taking his hand in hers and squeezing it briefly, she said

"Thank you for being discrete this evening."

They arrived at the hotel and Hollingsworth got out. She opened the driver's side window to say goodbye. She was tearing up again.

"They are going to fly you back to the States tomorrow. If things don't go well for Israel in the morning you won't be able to come back to the Middle East. Be safe!"

She rolled up her window and drove off. He went to his room and got very drunk. He was confused and very angry. The drunker he got, the more he hated Koudechah. He had taken Nicole away from him and didn't deserve her. He wallowed in self-pity until he fell asleep.

The four-hour war Israeli-Arab war

The Arab radar never detected the F35's coming. It wasn't until people on the ground heard the engines that the Arabs were alerted. The Stealth technology worked perfectly. The Arab fighters were nicely lined up to be fueled and armed for the upcoming attack which was planned in two days' time. The Iranians had insisted that the "Glorious Battle" begin on an appropriate Holy Day. Most of the bases lost three quarters of their aircraft on the first pass of the F35's. A few were scrambled and were airborne when the F16's arrived within minutes of the second attack by the F35's. Manned by inexperienced young pilots, they had strict orders to make the ground attack and run for home. The surviving Arab fighters thought they had scared the Israelis off. Then, the Israeli F16's arrived.

There was total confusion. The Arab radar systems mistook the Israeli F16's as friendly aircraft and they assumed that they were reinforcements from neighboring bases. The Israelis fired on their Arab foes mercilessly, assured by their IFF systems that they were enemy aircraft. The Arab pilots babbled on the AWACS radio frequencies that they couldn't tell friend from foe and started firing on fighters that showed up on their radar as friendly. It was chaos. Later, it was estimated that the Arabs shot down half of their own aircraft that had survived the F35 attack.

The remaining F16's in the first wave took out the AWACS and ground support radar systems in five different countries, all within two minutes. None had warning.

The second wave of F16's and A10 anti-tank aircraft that the Americans had discarded years ago, started the attack on the ground forces. The tanks were decimated and over 60,000 Arab soldiers died that day.

Koudechah was over the Iraq-Iran border and about to turn for home when his radar system went berserk. An enemy S27 had fired on him. The pilot must have realized that he was an enemy aircraft, despite his radar signals to the contrary. Koudechah instantly rolled the F16 inverted, pulled 9G into a vertical dive and lit the afterburners. Koudechah visualized the missile hurtling toward the ground after him and going much faster than his F16, which was approaching 1100 knots. At 2000 feet above the ground, Koudechah pulled the stick back with all the strength he could muster. Even with his G-suit almost crushing him, things started to go grey, a precursor to a complete blackout. He eased the back the pressure on the stick. His radar altimeter showed he was 800 feet above the ground.

The missile had caught up with the F16 but couldn't pull out sharply enough to hit Koudechah's plane. It passed below him and hit the ground a half kilometer ahead of the F16.

"Thank you, Henry," said Koudechah who had been told about the evasive maneuver by Hollingsworth. But the F16 flew directly through the debris from the missile explosion. At that speed there was no way to avoid it. Koudechah pulled up abruptly, the stick was shaking violently. The engine had flamed out. It took Koudechah less than a second to make the decision to eject.

"Fuck" He said in his best Anglo Saxon.

Suspended beneath his 'chute, he watched his aircraft disintegrate in mid-air and crash into the desert, bursting into flames on impact. He guided his parachute into a small clearing in the sagebrush and landed, unscathed.

He knew he had to get away from the wreckage before the Arabs found it. He didn't bother to go back to the plane, there would be nothing left of it. He started walking toward the Turkish border.

Hollingsworth became aware of the ringing telephone and his throbbing head at about the same time. He opened his eyes squinting at the sunlight streaming through the partially open curtain. It took several seconds for the unfamiliar surroundings to register.

The bedside lamp was still lit, the bottle of Johnny Walker, now nearly empty, stood by the telephone. He still wore his shirt unbuttoned and his tie hung loose around his neck. Memories of the events of the night before crept back into their places in his marinated brain, returning him to a state of throbbing consciousness.

"Jesus" He groaned to himself as he fumbled for the telephone.

"Hello" his own voice echoed in the earpiece. It sounded like a complete stranger.

"You sound awful" said the female voice on the phone.

It was Nicole, and he immediately felt his anger of last night burning inside him again.

"Why the hell would you care!" he spat back without thinking.

Nicole hesitated for a second and said quietly

"Have you seen the TV this morning?" she paused, half
expecting Andrew to hang up.

"Michel was shot down in the raid on Teheran this morning,
they think he ejected," she continued her voice trembling
slightly.

Hollingsworth didn't answer

"I. . ." She paused again, hoping for a response. "I just thought
you would want to know, that's all."

"I wouldn't give a shit if he'd got his head blown up his ass. If I
had known who he was when I first met him, I would have killed
the son of a bitch with my bare hands. I hope he rots in some
foul Arab jail for the rest of his miserable life!"

He hissed the last sentence into the phone with all the venom
he could muster and slammed the phone down knocking over
the bottle of Scotch.

"Shit" he screamed, picking up the bottle and throwing it into
the small metal waste basket with such force that it shattered.

"Shit! Shit! Shit!"

He flipped the TV on and lurched unsteadily toward the
bathroom. He sat on the Commode, his head cupped in both
palms and his elbows resting on his knees, peering at the TV
through the narrow opening in the doorway. His head felt as
though it was full of water and his eyes ached. He was aware of
having to make a conscious effort to focus on the TV.

Vivid pictures of Arab aircraft burning on the ground were being shown over and over again, as the announcer jabbered excitedly in Hebrew. A photograph of Koudechah, smiling happily with Nicole, filled the screen. Semitic writing scrolled underneath, and the announcer babbled on.

"Asshole!" Hollingsworth screamed at the TV, cringing at the pain which the noise of his own voice inflicted on him.

He showered and shaved and had begun to dress, when his still angry thoughts were interrupted by an authoritative rap on the door of the hotel room. Hollingsworth went to the door, opening it as far as the short security chain would allow. It occurred to him that, although the chain was heavy and strong, the screws which held it in place would easily be torn out by a well-developed 10-year-old pushing the door.

A uniformed Israeli Airforce officer stood outside the door.

"Good morning sir!"

Hollingsworth had to consciously redirect his foggy mind from the puzzle of the security chain.

"I'm here to take you to your plane sir. Colonel Koudechah orders sir."

Another memory of the previous night clicked into place. Koudechah had told him that he would arrange for him to be flown to Paris on an Israeli military flight chartered on UTA airlines.

"I'll be right there" Hollingsworth said, his voice still raspy and unfamiliar to himself.

"Right sir, shall I take your bags sir?"

"No, that's OK. I can manage thanks."

Hollingsworth closed the door, scrambled into his clothes and stuffed his belongings into the nylon parachute bag he used for carry-on. He was sweating profusely from the ill-effects of the alcohol and the hot shower. He called the front desk to get his bill prepared. After a few minutes of confusion with the Israeli desk clerk, a female voice came on the phone.

"Colonel Koudechah already took care of your bill sir. Just hand in your key at the front desk when you leave. I hope you had a pleasant stay, sir. Please come back and stay with us again next time you are in Tel Aviv."

The voice was smooth and calm, the English perfect with a classic BBC accent. Hollingsworth replied absently, thinking to himself "Don't these people know there is a fucking war on!"

He opened the door to leave, automatically glancing around the room for any forgotten item. He was surprised to find the young officer standing in exactly the same place.

"Ready Sir?" the officer reached out to take his bag.

"Oh yes, I am all set. Where are we catching the flight?" Hollingsworth couldn't recall Michel telling him where the plane departed from and he felt a little embarrassed.

"You have a seat on UTA 913 sir, it is a military charter departing Beersheba base at 11:30 hours. It's a two-hour drive so we need to hurry, sir." The officer stepped ahead to call the elevator.

The two men stood waiting for the elevator in silence both looking straight ahead at the pale enamel elevator doors. Hollingsworth's head still throbbed and he felt himself swaying slightly.

"Too bad about the Colonel, sir" The officer spoke directly to the elevator door.

"Yes" replied Hollingsworth, realizing that he actually meant it.

The elevator arrived and the Israeli ushered Hollingsworth inside, impatiently punching the button for the lobby. For the first time Hollingsworth made eye contact with his escort. He was a young lieutenant, clean-cut, his uniform neat and crisp.

"What happened exactly? I saw the news but I didn't understand enough Hebrew to really know what was going on from the video clips"

"Our fighters attacked in three waves. One group was deployed to attack the primary United Islamic fighter base to the North of Tehran. The other two groups knocked out the AWACS system and then hit the missile defense system they had installed along the Saudi border. Apparently, there was a lot of confusion amongst the Islamic forces, sir. Two separate fighter groups were deployed to protect the missile defense system but they mistook each other for the enemy, luckily for us. According to their own intelligence reports which we intercepted, eight UIA fighters were lost to friendly fire. Our F16's got the other six." It was clear from the young officer's assessment that he was unaware of the new IFF countermeasures which he had provided to the Israelis.

The young lieutenant was more relaxed now and related the rest of the events of the morning in perfect English with a very slight Boston accent. He had obviously been educated in the United States. Hollingsworth guessed he was in Military Security. He had clearly been well briefed in the events of the morning, probably with the expectation that Hollingsworth would want to know every detail.

"The Colonel was leading the third group which hit the base North of Tehran. Those Islamic bastards must have seen them coming despite the damage we inflicted on their AWACS. They had everything in the air waiting when Koudechah got there. They were outnumbered two to one. To make matters worse we lost two F16's to ground to air missiles on the way in."

"Apparently the S27s have some major problems with their IFF system because there was a lot of confusion there too. Lack of AWACS support made things worse; they had no airborne tactical coordination. If it hadn't been for these problems, they would have massacred us. As it was, we lost eight aircraft, five of these were direct hits, no survivors. Once the Arabs can figure out who to shoot at, they are deadly accurate.

Fortunately, there is no time to figure out who is friend and who is foe so wound up downing at least six of their own aircraft."

"The colonel was lucky." The lieutenant continued. "He was fired upon but was less than 5000 feet above the terrain. He chaffed out and went right down on the deck, to try to confuse the missile radar with ground reflections. But the missile had heat guidance as well. According to his wingman, the missile hit the ground a few hundred meters in front of him. He must have collected most of the debris in the intake and flamed out. Colonel Koudechah punched out just before the fighter hit the ground and exploded. His wingman reported seeing the 'chute open but was too high to check if Koudechah was OK and didn't have enough fuel to go down and take a look. They will probably send a chopper in for him tonight.

The elevator reached the lobby.

"How many S27's did the UIA lose?" Hollingsworth asked?

"Twenty-three" was the quick response.

"How many did they have?"

"Twenty-three" replied the lieutenant allowing himself a very slight grin.

Hollingsworth smiled for the first time since he had staggered out of bed that morning. He handed his room key to the attractive young lady at the front desk.

"Have a nice trip home Mr. Hollingsworth" Miss BBC smiled broadly, obviously proud of her perfect English accent.

The lieutenant ushered Hollingsworth out through the side door of the hotel lobby. A black Mercedes sedan, parked on the other side of the street with the motor running, drew up silently to the curb near the door. The car was driven be a middle-aged civilian in a chauffeur's uniform. The lieutenant opened the rear door of the car for Hollingsworth.

"Do you have your papers sir? The papers you were given upon your arrival that is."

Hollingsworth was surprised at the question and fumbled in his inside jacket pocket for several minutes. He handed them to the officer.

"And your passport please" The officer was more formal now, more authoritative. The lieutenant studied Hollingsworth passport very carefully, checking every page. He handed the passport back to Hollingsworth then folded the entry documents precisely in half then in half again. He put then in the top pocket of his uniform which he carefully re-buttoned.

"Sorry for all the formality sir but at times like these a little formality can sometimes be the difference between life and death. You will only need your passport to board the aircraft. Even the American authorities will not know that you have visited Israel. The fewer people who know you were here the better, for you and for Israel I think."

"Of course," said Hollingsworth offering his hand to the young man. The officer shook his hand and saluted Hollingsworth informally, closed the car door and bent to the open window.

"Sorry we couldn't arrange the SR72 for your trip back sir." The lieutenant now smiled broadly.

"Colonel Koudechah told us that we wouldn't have had a chance without your help sir. I would like to thank you personally for coming to Israel, particularly since it isn't your fight sir."

"You would be surprised lieutenant, you'd be surprised!" replied Hollingsworth raising his window as the officer motioned the car away.

Hollingsworth leaned back into the plush leather seat of the Mercedes and closed his eyes. It occurred to him how incongruous it was to be sitting in a luxury German car in the middle of Israel just 3 generations after Hitler had murdered six million Jews. He was soon dozing fitfully, tired of watching the teeming life of Tel Aviv through the tinted windows of the car.

Nicole quietly replaced the telephone receiver in its cradle, tears welling in her eyes.

"Damn him!" she exclaimed out loud. She sat down on the arm of the small sofa, dejected, thinking to herself, "Why are men always such children? Why does Andrew suddenly hate the man with whom he has become such close friends, just because he finds out that he is married to me?" She tilted her head back, closing her eyes to fight the tears, trying not to think of Michel but unable to contemplate anything else.

The front door bell chimed graciously. She rose apprehensively, very conscious that any bad news about Michel would be brought to her personally. Through the window, she could see the Airforce staff car parked in the street. Her heart sank and she bit her bottom lip subconsciously. She crossed the broad hallway and, hesitating for a moment, drew a deep breath and opened the door. Colonel Zabros stood at the door, his hands hung down in front of him, fiddling with his peaked military hat.

"You've seen the news Nicole? He asked solemnly.

"Yes, of course." She ushered Zabros into the large sunlit living room where she and Michel had laughed with this same Colonel and his pretty wife on many occasions. For the first time in her life she suddenly felt that she might not be able to deal with what was happening to her.

"We don't know much Nicole." Zabros' voice was almost a whisper his words, unwittingly coming as stunning relief to her.

"Then he is not..." Her voice trailed off. She had to force herself to utter the words.

"He's not dead then?" she had expected the worst from a personal visit from the Air Force commander.

"We don't honestly know Nicole. We got two independent reports from the crews that he ejected and that his 'chute opened. But one of the aircraft in the vicinity was so low on fuel that the pilot could not stay to verify that Michel was ok. The other aircraft was at 8,000 meters altitude, far too high to get a visual. We are waiting for some satellite pictures of the area. They may tell us something."

The colonel put his hat down on the coffee table.

"I would have come earlier, Nicole, but we've been trying to get all the information we can. My guess is that since the 'chute opened, he's probably OK unless he was hit by shrapnel before he punched out. "

"Oh God Levi," she said, her face crumpling.

Zabros Took her in his arms, quickly stroking her hair, closer now to her then maybe he had ever been to anyone even his own wife. Now she finally allowed her tears to come, and abandoned herself to the involuntary sobbing that now wracked her body. Zabros held her very close, fighting tears himself until, after a few minutes, the convulsion stopped and she gently pushed him away. The front of his uniform was dark from her tears.

Nicole visibly gathered herself together. Wiping away the tears, smoothing her hair and patting at her nose with a crumpled tissue, she said,

"Thank God they sent you, Levi. I'm such a mess." She smiled at him with the easy affection of old friends. "Can I get you a drink?"

"Yes, but make it a light one. I'm on duty "

He came up behind her while she was fixing the drinks and gently put his arm around her shoulders. He searched desperately for an easy way to say what he had to say.

"I'm afraid that's the good news Nicole, the rest is not so good.

"He's out of range of the rescue helicopters, and even if he was within range, the choppers would never make it through the ground defenses near the border and they can't get high enough to get above them."

"Can't they send a plane in to get him?" pleaded Nicole.

"No, the terrain is pretty bad, there is nowhere to land an aircraft out there. "

"Are they going to send in troops then?" Her voice was quavering now.

"No, if we send in paratroops, we have to we have no way to get them out again, for the same reasons that we can't get to Michel. The top brass won't risk a ground-based rescue mission. The odds are just not good enough to risk so many lives for one man, particularly when you don't even know if he has made it."

Nicole's face turned ashen. With her hair disheveled and her make up the streaked from tears, she suddenly looked much older than her 30 years.

"You can't just leave him there; you know what they do to captured it is Israeli pilots."

Her voice was shrill, Zabros knew that she was close to breaking again.

"God! Please tell me you're just won't leave him there. "

Her hands were tight little fists, held up close to her face and her voice was still shrill. Her eyes pleaded with his, burning into his soul. He knew they wouldn't risk much to rescue one man, but he couldn't bring himself to tell her that. He didn't want to hear the words himself.

"We're going to send in a fighter to drop medical supplies food and weapons as soon as we get a fix on his position. "

"Doesn't he have a locator beacon in his parachute pack?"

She and Michel had often discussed would happen if he had to bail out in an emergency.

He told her about the emergency systems so that she wouldn't worry so much about his flying. But that was in peacetime.

"Yes, he does," Zabros concurred," but he knows that if he turns it on the Arabs will locate it and they will get to him before we do. "

"They will know where he is if they drop supplies for him, won't they?" Her eyes questioning him.

"Maybe." Zabros had to avert his eyes from her. There was a long uncomfortable silence. Zabros scrutinized his drink, bracing himself for her inevitable question.

"He won't make it back, will he? "

She looked at him for a long time and then, before he could respond, she said quietly into her drink,

"I think it would have been better if you had told me he was dead." She began to cry again. This time the tears were just streaming silently down her face. He took her drink from her hand and set it down on the table with his own and cradled her in his arms. He felt weak and helpless.

"If he's not hurt, he'll make it. Christ, he's taught the desert survival class for the last five years. He's fitter than most of the younger pilots. He'll make it to the mountains and when he gets close enough, we'll go in and get him. "

He kept up the banter of reassurances until she pushed herself away from him again.

"Go now Levi. I'd like to be alone. I'll be OK. Call me when you know more than CNN does. "

He was hurt by her sarcasm. He held onto her for a moment - facing her, holding her at arms-length by the shoulders. She looked up at him, her eyes searching his face as if to find some hidden truth. Then she said quietly, "Don't tell me to hang in there Levi, just go back there and tell those ungrateful bastards to do something. Now!"

With that she broke her gaze and reclaimed her glass from the counter where he had set it.

The phone rang as Zabros let himself out. It was the Press. A man claiming to be from the Jerusalem Post asked to speak to Madame Zabros. He gave his name.

"She isn't home at the moment. I'll tell her you called." Nicole responded politely in Hebrew and hung up. She knew how to deal with the press, she was one of them.

She went into the bedroom and quickly packed a small bag. As she was leaving the room, she glanced at the picture of her husband in the small silver frame on the bedside table. It had been taken on the day Michel had graduated from flight school. He was standing next to a single-seat military jet, his flight helmet under his arm, grinning from ear to ear. He was twenty-two. She slipped the photograph out of its frame and put it in her purse.

The back door of the townhouse led to a sunny brick courtyard which served as a parking area for the five tenants of the building. The bougainvillea was in full bloom and its scent filled the air. She glanced up as usual, to check that she had closed the bedroom windows which overlooked the courtyard. Her yellow e-type Jaguar was parked under the bedroom balcony. A small marmalade cat rushed out from under the car to greet her, but she hadn't the time for it today. It scampered away confused.

The Jag finally started on the third try and she cursed the British and their cars in coarse French. She backed up and got out of the car to open the wrought iron gates to the court-yard and then drove off, leaving the gates open. The other tenants would complain once again but she was in a hurry. She glanced at her watch. She would be lucky to make it to the base at Mitzpe Ramon before Andrew's plane left.

She liked to drive the e-type and could do so better than Michel, although he would never admit to it. Now she snaked through the interminable traffic of Tel Aviv like a veteran cab driver. Michel had taught her to drive. She had never owned a car in Paris, it wasn't necessary. "Anticipate," he had drummed it into her. You have to be in the right gear at the right time. Now she did it without thinking.

She edged out onto Hayarkon opposite the French embassy and made a left, squealing the tires in second gear. The speed limit was 60 kph, but she pushed the Jag up to 100 between the Frishman and Allenby intersections. She had to get to the highway in ten minutes or she would never make it. The next intersection was backed up with traffic, so she made an abrupt left turn across the bows of a furious taxi driver coming up on the inside lane. She hurtled through the back streets, coming out on Harkavet. The main highway through the heart of Tel Aviv was now in sight. She passed an old Peugeot and a truck ambling down the on-ramp, and by the time she passed the Tel Aviv railway station she was doing 200 kph.

When she used to drive with Michel, he would keep up a constant barrage of instructions; "Shift down... get around this cornichon. . .!" On one spring day they rented a classic Citroen SM to drive down to Lyon for a wedding. Michel was keeping up his usual stream of instructions as they wound through the traffic on the Route Peripherique onto the A6 highway. She maneuvered smoothly into the fast lane and put her foot down... 120 kph, 150, 170 - at 200kph Michel finally shut up.

"Thank you" she said, putting her foot down all the way and enjoying the surge of power delivered by the 3-liter Maserati V6 engine.

From that day onwards Michel ceased the barrage, preferring instead to bury his head in the newspaper or a book. She reached Beer Shiva in less than an hour. She tried to visualize where Michel was now, to see through his eyes, see what he saw. She knew in her heart that he was still alive. She would have felt him cry out to her if he was gone.

"God, please don't let them capture him," she found herself praying for the first time in her life. She HAD to get to the base before Andrew's plane left. The Israeli government owed Andrew an unrepayable debt. They would listen to him. Only he could persuade them to go in after Michel. What would she do if he wouldn't talk to her? What would she do if he left anyway? The faster her thoughts raced, the faster she drove.

"God, please make him listen to me." She was praying again.

The Jag was getting hot. The water temperature was in the red zone and she was nearly out of gas.

"Merde!" she said to herself, backing off the throttle just enough to slide into a gap in the traffic and slip down the exit ramp, still doing well over 120 kph. She pulled into the Total petrol station and stopped. The throaty burble of the Jag's exhaust echoed under the canopy over the fuel pumps. She turned off the ignition and spoke to the young attendant.

"Fill me up with everything: oil, petrol and water. Quickly please, I'm in a hurry."

"Anything else I can fill you up with lady?"

She looked down at the object of the attendant's prurient interest and realized that her pencil skirt had ridden up exposing her slip and the tops of her very French hose. She blushed slightly and, putting on her best throaty French accent she levelled her eyes directly at the attendant's crotch and said "Keep it in your pants big boy!"

The young attendant blushed crimson and scurried off to get the oil.

While the car was being refueled, she bought a map and located the airbase. She had been there once before with Michel but, like most passengers, she hadn't paid attention to the route he had taken, and there was no GPS in the car. She remembered that, for security reasons, there were no signposts to the base on the highway. She would have to leave the highway about 5 kilometers south. From there it was about 120 kilometers, kleeks, as Michel called them. She would have to slow down once she got off the highway. It would take nearly an hour. She looked at her watch. She would be lucky to make it.

She paid the attendant and slid sensuously back behind the wheel of the low car, deliberately allowing her skirt to ride all the way up. The attendant averted his eyes this time.

She pressed the starter and the Jag roared back to life. It always started immediately when it was hot.

"Ciao Bambino!" she grinned at the boy over the open window and let the clutch out, spraying gravel from the rear tires. The Jag growled loudly in first gear.

By the time she reached the airbase access road, the back of her blouse was soaked in perspiration and the car was getting hot again. It had taken less than 45 minutes.

The base was surrounded by a high chain-link fence, topped with coils of barbed wire. A lower fence without barbed wire ran parallel, four of five meters inside. Rhodesian Ridgeback dogs, trained to kill, patrolled the space between the fences. Beyond the inner fence, high towers, spaced two-hundred-and-fifty meters apart, formed another line 25 meters inside. Michel had told her that the space between the dog run and the towers was strewn with anti-tank mines. Each tower was manned 24 hours a day by four guards equipped with night goggles, 50 caliber machine guns and RPGs. An enemy attack would be a costly affair.

The single entrance gate was flanked by two towers. In the center of the four-lane entrance road was a low, sand-colored guard- house from which extended long yellow-and-black-striped steel barriers, blocking both lanes in each direction. The barriers looked heavy enough to stop a tank.

As Nicole approached the gate, the entrance barrier was sliding back on its rail to permit the Mercedes to pass through. It had to be Andrews's car. The Israeli army didn't let too many people make use of limousines. She couldn't see the occupants through the dark tinted windows, but she knew it must be his.

An armed guard in desert-camouflage fatigues was motioning her to stop. She was still going pretty fast. The guard stepped slightly to the side, unconsciously bringing his weapon to bear on the car, not sure it was going to stop. She screeched to a halt alongside the guardhouse, just a little too far forward so that the guard could not close the barrier without crushing her car.

She fumbled in her purse for her press pass. The guard who had been waving her down approached from behind. She could see the barrel of his weapon in the rear-view mirror on her side of the car. The second guard now brought his weapon to bear on her from the other side of the car. She flashed the press card at the first guard.

"I'm Colonel Koudechah's wife." She said almost breathless. "I'm with Mr. Hollingsworth's party." She turned her head to look the guard directly in the eyes, ignoring the weapon which was now so close to her face that she could smell the machine oil that the guard had used to clean it before coming on duty. She was already putting the press pass back in her purse.

The guard relaxed, lowering the weapon instinctively, recognition in his eyes. He had seen her on television that day.

"Sorry to hear about your husband Mrs K." he spoke in Hebrew, abbreviating her husband's name with a certain reverence. " Don't worry we'll have him out of there in no time. I know that they flew a reconnaissance sortie out of here today. We'll get him back. Don't you worry"

With that, the guard stepped back and waved her through.

"Thank you" she said sincerely in Hebrew, easing the car away slowly, half expecting the guard to realize that she hadn't shown him a valid gate pass and would come running after her. If he did, she decided, she was just going to keep going, pretending not to hear or see him.

She had kept her eye on the Mercedes and had seen it turn right behind some buildings just ahead. She turned at the same place and found herself on a huge concrete apron in front of a row of hangars, in front of which were parked various military transport aircraft. One plane stood out. It was a commercial passenger jet in faded UTA colors.

The Mercedes was already parked in front of it. She could hear the whine of the jet engines and saw that a mobile jet-way was rolled up to the front passenger door. A stewardess in UTA uniform stood in the open doorway, her blonde hair blowing in the brisk wind. Andrew was getting a bag out of the trunk as she pulled the Jag up alongside the Mercedes.

"What the hell are you doing here?" Andrew grunted, reluctant to speak at all. He didn't have to ask why she had come and he would rather have ignored her altogether, but he couldn't. The Jaguar was blocking his path to the plane.

"You're wasting your time, "he said turning on his heel and striding off around the Mercedes towards the plane. Nicole got out of her car and ran after him, her high heels clicking on the windswept concrete.

"Andrew! Please listen to me!." she shouted at him, against the wind and above the shriek of the jet engines.

He stopped and turned toward her. She didn't give him a chance to speak.

"You are the only one who can help him, Andrew, they're going to leave him in the desert to die or, even worse, to be captured by the Arabs. Do you know what they did with the last Israeli pilot they caught?" Again, she didn't give him a chance to respond.

"They chained him naked to a stake in the center of the village where they captured him. The villagers stoned him every day and then urinated and defecated on him. At night the dogs would come and tear pieces of flesh from his body and eat it. The villagers stopped the dogs from killing him and it was three days before he died. Then they let the dogs have him. Do you want that to happen to your friend?"

"He's not my friend!" Hollingsworth hissed.

"He was before you found out he was married to me. Why won't you stay here and help him? The government owes you for what you did for them, for Israel. They will listen to you. You know that, and there is absolutely no reason why you have to leave right now, is there?"

"No there isn't, "he screamed, infuriated even further by her undeniable feminine logic.

"Why in Hell should I help him? He treated you like shit, he deserves everything he gets.

"There was fury in Hollingsworth's eyes now and Nicole knew she had to turn him now or never.

"Yes, he did treat me badly ". Her voice was calm now.

"But that's not why you hate him is it? You hate him because you're jealous. I forgave him his indiscretions because I was partly to blame for them and because I love him."

Now, she let her rage surface, her eyes blazing at his, a slender finger pointed accusingly at his face.

"You're prepared to let a man you called your friend, die just because you are jealous prick. I will never forgive you for that as long as I live!" She turned to leave, and he caught her arm.

"OK! "he said. "I'll stay and talk to them. But that's all. "

"Thank you. "Hollingsworth saw her mouth the words but couldn't hear them above the noise of the jet. He let go of her; she walked back to her car and sat in the driver's seat, leaning her head back against the headrest. She felt drained. She wanted to let the sense of relief washed over, but she knew the battle to get Michel back had only just begun. She closed her eyes.

Hollingsworth dismissed the driver of the Mercedes with instructions to inform the Lieutenant that he had decided to stay in Tel Aviv, and then went up the gangway to the plane. The stewardess greeted him with a plastic smile.

"Bon! Vous etes pret a partir Monsieur? Nous avons vous entendu." The stewardess's tone of voice made it obvious that she wasn't happy that they had been waiting for him for some time. But she retained the plastic smile anyway.

"I am sorry, but I won't be boarding," Hollingsworth told the young woman. "There has been a change of plans."

The smile faded instantly. The stewardess muttered to herself, spoke into a small radio in her hand, and turned to attend to the door. She made it obvious that there was no further need for communication with him. The ground crew was ready to remove the gangway as soon as he stepped off. He gave them a slight nod of thanks and strode over to the Jag. Settling himself into the passenger seat he said.

"That stewardess called me a cornichon, does that mean what I think it means?"

"Yes, she thinks you're a prick, too."

She drove back to Tel Aviv at a more leisurely pace. There was little conversation. The long silences were separated by a few questions from Andrew and fragmented answers from Nicole. By the time they reached the outskirts of Tel Aviv, Hollingsworth knew as much as Nicole, which wasn't a lot. The information from the guard about the reconnaissance flight was really the only thing he didn't already know. They had to find out if Koudechah was still alive, but he couldn't put it that way to Nicole.

"We have to find out what they got from reconnaissance sortie first. Who do we talk to? "Hollingsworth asked.

"He's not dead, if that's what you mean!" she glanced at him, knowing exactly what the question implied. "I would know if he was."

"Levi will know if they've found him. We should have checked my message machine at home to see if he telephoned. I don't think he has my mobile number." They pulled into a small shopping area, and Nicole called her home from her mobile phone. Hollingsworth stood behind her, and after what seemed like an eternity, she exclaimed,

"Merde"

"What is it?" Hollingsworth asked anxiously.

"The Press, they must call every five minutes, every one of them." Then, she went rigid. She had stopped breathing, the phone pressed hard to her ear, her eyes closed. She opened her eyes suddenly. They shone through a mist of tears.

"They've found him Andrew! They've found him and he's alright! Oh thank God! Here, listen, I'll rewind it."

She pressed a button on her phone, handed it to Andrew, and stood, watching his eyes. Hollingsworth listened intently for a few minutes and then gave the phone back to her.

"According to that message, he must be moving pretty fast. Call Levi and tell him we need to talk to him. Maybe he can get us in to see Gibli. He's the only person able to make the decision."

"No." retorted Nicole abruptly. "Levi has no guts. Let's go directly to the Department of Defense offices. Gibli will see you. He has to."

The got back in the car and threaded their way through the suburbs of Tel Aviv toward the ocean. Nicole turned on the radio, dividing her attention between watching the road and twiddling the radio dial from one station to another, looking for a news broadcast. The radio was as old as the car and didn't have a 'scan' function. When the pointer reached the end of the dial, she punched the off button in disgust.

"Alors! They are more interested in the latest scandal in parliament than in the war." She slumped back in her seat and concentrated on her driving again. Hollingsworth picked up the road map of Israel that Nicole had bought at the gas station and began to study it. Israel, he thought to himself, was now surrounded on three sides by belligerent enemies, and on the fourth side, by the Mediterranean Sea. How long would it be before another attempt was made to drive the Israelis into the sea?

The sun was sinking into the Mediterranean as Nicole parked in front of the Defense Department building.

"I think you should go in alone, Andrew," said Nicole. I think he is more likely to be open with you if I'm not there. I'll go home and make something to eat. You can get a cab at the hotel across the street when you're through."

"Ok." There wasn't much else he could say. He knew that part of the reason she didn't want to go in with him was because she would get angry again.

"I'll do my best," he said.

"I know" she said, touching him gently, her eyes lingering on his for a moment.

"Bonne chance" she said smiling up at him through the car window.

He could still hear the guttural exhaust of the Jag as she shifted down to turn the corner at the end of the street. He straightened his tie, and with an air of easy authority he strode through the double glass doors of the ministry building.

It took nearly an hour, working with the security officer on the telephone, before he had worked his way up through the ranks of the bureaucracy to Gibli's secretary. She was the only one who knew who he was. She immediately came down to the security area to get him.

She ushered him into Gibli's office. In complete contrast to the austere décor of the building, the room was tastefully furnished in beautiful Louis XIV antiques. A thick oriental rug incongruously covered the cheap tile floor. The large windows overlooked the city onto the Mediterranean, now black except for a few twinkling lights from boats heading up and down the coast. Gibli rose to meet him.

"Andrew!" The minister stretched out a suntanned hand in greeting. "I thought you were on your way back to Washington."

"I was until I heard about Colonel Koudechah."

The minister put his head around the office door and spoke briefly to his secretary. Hollingsworth sat down in one of the rich leather armchairs facing the minister's desk. Gibli sat down behind the desk and lit a cigarette, offering one to Hollingsworth.

Hollingsworth held up a hand in refusal.

"A great show, as you Brits would say. We lost a lot of aircraft, but not nearly as many as we would have done without your help, Andrew. We wiped out their fleet of MDFs and destroyed their AWACs resources completely. They lost three aircraft to every one of our losses. A total rout! I don't think they'll be back anytime soon.

"Did you know that we have found the Colonel?" Gibli continued. "We sent out a fast reconnaissance aircraft with infrared cameras. Three separate missions an hour apart. All of them spotted him. He's making for the mountains."

"Yes, I know, Colonel Zabros informed me. We have to get him out of there before the Arabs get him."

"Is that why you are here?" asked Gibli

"Yes" Hollingsworth nodded. "Exactly"

The secretary came in with coffee. Gibli remained silent while his secretary served the coffee.

"You won't find too many American secretaries doing that anymore" said Hollingsworth after she left, closing the door behind her.

"That is true," said Gibli, "and yet I believe women have enjoyed equality in Israel since the beginning. They fight in our army, have led our government, and hold, proportionately, many more positions of power and influence in the public sector than is the case in the USA. There is no 'old boy's network' in Israel my friend. We use the best talent we can get, male or female.

"So long as it's Jewish and not Palestinian" quipped Hollingsworth.

Gibli's smile faded a little. He was not about to discuss the treatment of the Palestinians with a British engineer. He chose to ignore Hollingsworth's comment and continued, "I was briefed by the chiefs of staff less than two hours ago. Why don't we go into the briefing room and I'll acquaint you with the facts as we know them" Gibli rose, taking his coffee with him, and led Hollingsworth into the adjacent room.

The briefing room was dominated by a huge colored relief map of the Middle East covering the entire end-wall. A large conference-room table sat in the center of the room, surrounded by ten high-backed chairs. The floor, tiled in the same drab beige as Gibli's office, was bare and well scuffed. A projector lens protruded from a square opening above the map. A large pull-down screen covered most of the wall at the other end of the room, except for the door through which they had entered.

"Make yourself comfortable. I'll get someone up here to run the projector." He picked up the phone in the corner of the room and spoke a few words of Hebrew to the person on the other end of the line.

For the next two hours Hollingsworth listened to Gibli cover every aspect of the situation. The Israelis had the strengths and positions of the various Muslim and Arab forces, supply-movements, and strategic communications intelligence gleaned from satellite- and VHF-eavesdropping. All of it was up-to-the-minute, verified by multiple sources and, in most cases, supported by high-altitude and satellite-reconnaissance, which Hollingsworth could now see was as good as or even better than anything the Americans had, and a lot better organized. It was obvious that the United Islamic State had intended to mount a major offensive.

The picture was much more recent than the satellite pictures he had been shown earlier. The Syrians had moved forward, along the border of the UN buffer zone to the East of the Golan Heights. A buildup of Jordanian troops had taken place all along the East bank of the Jordan River. Saudi Muslims, led by the victorious rebels responsible for the grisly death of the Saudi Royal family, were already in the Sinai desert, ready to confront Israel. There could be no doubt that if the UIA had gained air superiority over Israel, they would have launched the largest ground-attack against Israel in the modern history of the Middle East.

It was also clear that although the Israeli forces were formidable, it was unlikely that they could sustain a ground-defense on all fronts without help from outside. Hollingsworth interrupted Gibli.

"What happens if the Arabs launch the ground-attack anyway? You can't possibly defend yourselves on all fronts simultaneously. Can you?"

"No, Andrew, we can't, but let me show you something else" Gibli picked up the phone again, and a few minutes later a film began rolling on the screen. A red line ran down the middle of the screen, followed by a jumble of letters and numbers, then a submarine bearing the Star of David on the conning tower crystalized on the screen. The vessel submerged gracefully, leaving barely a ripple on the surface of the placid water.

Seconds later, four enormous plumes of water erupted into the air, from which emerged dull brown cylinders topped with white nose-caps. They moved rapidly up and down the screen as the camera operator struggled to pan the camera fast enough to keep the missiles in the center of the viewfinder.

"We conducted these tests in the Indian Ocean nearly five years ago" Gibli announced, with little emotion.

"The Americans thought it was the Russians testing their SS3s and the Russians thought it was the Americans testing their latest ICBM after the Nuclear Cruise missiles were banned". Gibli lit another cigarette.

"We've come a long way since then. The range of these weapons is now well over 7500 kilometers at Mach 3·5, with accuracy of 25 meters at maximum range, better if we have GPS coordinates of the target. Each missile can carry three [independently- targeted warheads of 50 megatons each. We have eleven of those subs out there somewhere." Gibli waved his cigarette in the direction of the Mediterranean, that was visible through the window.

"They are so stealthy we can't even find them ourselves! Each sub carries 24 missiles with designated targets and orders to fire them if all communication with Tel Aviv is lost.". Gibli stubbed out his cigarette in the already-full ashtray.

The screen now showed designated targets of the Israeli strategic missile system: Damascus, Baghdad, Hama, Halas, Najaf, As Basra, Teheran…, the list went on and on. Every major city in Iraq, Iran, Jordan, Syria and Libya was targeted by multiple nuclear warhead ballistic missiles launched from Israeli submarines in the Mediterranean. It would take ten minutes for the Israeli missiles to reach Baghdad. The last crusade against the Muslim hordes would last less than fifteen minutes.

"You are the only person outside the Israeli Military Intelligence who has ever seen this film, Andrew. I am showing it to you so that you know what a debt Israel and all of the Middle East owes you. I have little doubt that, if we had been unable to maintain air superiority yesterday, the UIA would have invaded on all fronts and Israel would be forced to unleash these terrible weapons. We owe you a lot, Andrew, but I can't repay that debt by wittingly ordering the Army to send people to their certain death.

Gibli now stood at the wall map.

"Koudechah is here" he stabbed at the map with a short wooden pointer at North Eastern corner of Iraq.

"He went down about here" he stabbed again.

"He is moving at four to five kilometers per hour over some pretty rough terrain, so he is obviously not hurt, not seriously anyway. He is making for the Turkish border. We have attack and rescue helicopters here in Israel but they are barely within range. We would have to fly over Syria and Iraq to get to him. Thanks to you, we can provide them with fighter cover, but the chances of the choppers getting past the ground defenses are virtually nil. The Muslims are armed with French ground-to-air missiles that are effective against supersonic aircraft, let alone choppers flying at 300 knots. We would probably lose them all."

"Can't you fly the choppers out of Turkey?" asked Hollingsworth. "They are neutral, aren't they?"

"The Turks haven't joined the UIA. They were a founding member of the UN and don't want to jeopardize their seat. They won't permit us to fly military operations from Turkey because they don't want to piss off the UIA, but we can fly civilian and transport planes into Turkey. They are walking a very fine political line.

"So, Koudechah has to get to the Turkish border before the Arabs get him. We can't send in ground forces with air support from Turkey to get him out. If he doesn't get to the border, he's toast. He is well respected by his men and by Zabros, his commanding officer. If we lose him like this it will have a terrible impact on morale as well as being a tragic loss. Believe me, I know how you feel, but there is nothing we can do unless he gets to Turkey."

"What do you think the chances are that he will get there before the Arabs find him?"

"Nil" said Gibli. "They must already know roughly where he is. They have already put a couple of choppers in the air with infrared detectors. It's a huge area to search, but they'll find him within three or four days at the most. Even if he walks all day and night for four days at five kph, that would still put him out of range, and it would be impossible, even for him, to keep up that pace."

"What about going in with a light reconnaissance aircraft or something like that?" asked Hollingsworth.

"No way! We would have to overfly Syria and Iraq. A light aircraft would be just as visible on radar and just as vulnerable to missile fire as the choppers. Besides, the range is still a problem."

"Not for a glider it isn't."

"A glider?" Gibli was incredulous. "This is not a time for humor Andrew. You can't be serious."

"I am!" Hollingsworth snapped back." The Airforce Flying Club owns a two-seat motor glider. It's made of carbon fiber and virtually invisible on radar. It has a glide ratio of 60 to one, which means it will fly nearly a hundred and eighty miles from a height of 15,000 feet. The retractable engine is powerful enough to take off, even from high altitude fields, and has a range of 1300 miles on only 15 gallons of fuel. Not only that, it will fly at 150 knots, faster than many light planes, and you can land it in a football field."

"What are you getting at?" said Gibli, curious now, but still doubtful.

"If we could get that glider to here." Hollingsworth stabbed the map. "We could aero-tow the glider somewhere over the Urals at night and release it at 15,000 feet above the ground about here, just before dawn. Then we would glide silently to about here." He pointed at the map again. "Then we put the engine out, climb back to 15,000, and glide again. We do that several times until we get within reach of where the colonel will be in another 24 hours. They wouldn't see us on radar, and the chances of being seen from the ground after daybreak are pretty slim."

"What do you mean aero-tow?" Gibli realized that Hollingsworth was serious and that his plan was beginning to look plausible.

"Gliders have a hook in the front. Even motor gliders have this so they can be towed by another aircraft. Aero-towing the motor glider would preserve the limited amount of fuel it can carry, instead of burning it up to take off and climb to altitude using the retractable motor." He showed Gibli a picture on his iPhone of his own motor glider with the engine extended.

"So that way you can fly more than 1300 miles."

"Yes, but we also have to get back." The 'we' wasn't lost on Gibli, but he chose to ignore it for the moment.

"So how do you propose to get back?" Gibli was listening intently now, sensing that, perhaps, this wild idea might be a viable solution.

"Gliders are built to use thermals, columns of hot air rising off the ground like dust devils. I am sure you have seen hawks or vultures circling in them. In desert conditions it is not unusual to be able to climb at 1000 ft per minute to 15,000 or 20,000 feet. In contrast, a single engine Cessna is barely capable of climbing at 500 ft per minute. We would refuel with the gas cans that can be loaded in the glider in place of the rear passenger. Then we would take off and climb straight ahead until we found another thermal. Once at the top of the thermal, we simply glide at 80 knots toward the mountains. We find another thermal and repeat the process.

"What happens if you don't find another thermal?" Gibli was looking at him now trying to gauge how realistic this completely unconventional idea really was."

"Then we deploy the engine and use the rest of the fuel to climb back up."

"Is there enough fuel to get you back without thermals?"

"No" Hollingsworth was factual. The glider would not make it back without using thermals. But in desert conditions there was usually an abundant supply of heat that causes the thermals to kick off.

"Are you really serious Andrew? Do you think that this could really succeed?" Gibli was looking him in the eyes, looking for any doubt.

"I'm not going to say it is easy, because it isn't. If the sailplane is damaged on landing in rough terrain then we will never get it off the ground. We're toast. If we do get it off the ground, we have a good chance of getting to the mountains. If everything goes exactly right, we'll get home. The point is that you are risking only one glider and one person to try this. The odds are not bad for the risks involved. The alternative seems to be that you leave him there to die."

Hollingsworth started to explain how the wind can affect the thermals and make it harder to gain altitude.

"I don't want to know all the technicalities, Andrew. What are the chances you can get both of you back within range of our ground forces? No bullshit, what are the odds? Are they good enough for you to fly this mission yourself? You know damn well we don't have anybody else here who could do it." Gibli was very serious now and stood facing Hollingsworth, looking directly into his eyes.

"Yes sir!" Hollingsworth had already decided to do it even if Gibli didn't agree. His real motivation was that he wanted to make Nicole happy.

"What do you need," said Gibli, picking up the phone.

The secretary came in with more coffee, and the young Lieutenant came into the room. Gibli introduced him.

"Lieutenant Ephron, this is Mr. Hollingsworth. I believe you two have met."

For the next two hours, the three men planned the operation in detail. The glider would be disassembled and put in its trailer by Airforce club members. A C130 transport plane would pick up the glider and take it and Ephron to the launch site at Fik airfield, on the West shore of the Sea of Galilee. A Polish Wilga plane located at the Fik was scheduled to make the tow. Andrew would be flown there early in the morning.

It was time to get some sleep.

"Can I drop you somewhere?" asked Gibli.

"Yes, I promised Madame Koudechah that I would let her know what was going on."

Fifteen minutes later Hollingsworth was at the front door of the Koudechah's townhouse. The place was in darkness. Nicole came to the door wearing the robe he had bought her in Lyon. She had obviously been sleeping.

"I had given up on you" she said, "I ate already and went to bed. I thought they may have deported you or that you had gone home to America." She switched on the lights in the living room and drew the drapes. He flopped down on the sofa, realizing he was dog tired. It had been a bloody long day!

"Would you like a drink?"

"A beer if you have one, please."

"The longer I waited, the less chance I thought that you would get them to do anything. Are they going to go in after him?" She handed him the beer and sat on the sofa beside him, her legs curled up under her. She was staring at him intently.

"No," he said. "I am"

"You can't be serious!" Nicole was completely taken aback.

"There's no other way." Hollingsworth explained the situation to her and what they planned to do. She re-filled her champagne glass a couple of times while talked, but he refused another beer aware that, in the morning, he would need all the wit he could muster.

When he finished, he rose and said "They're sending a car for me at 2:30 in the morning, so I had better get some sleep. I hope you don't mind, but I took the liberty of telling them that I was going to stay here. "I'll crash on the sofa."

She stood up too, facing him and puttting her glass down on the side-table.

"I can't let you do this Andrew. I didn't expect you to get involved. All I wanted was for you to persuade them to make the effort to get him back. I don't want you to risk your life too.

Call them now and tell them it's off. Call them now!"

"There is no other way Nicole. You can see that. Besides, it's already nearly midnight, they've all gone home" He smiled down at her, trying to keep things light-hearted. She put her arms around him and drew herself to him, holding him very tight with her hands flat against his warm back.

"God! What have I done?" she asked into his shirt.

He took her by the shoulders, pushing her away gently, so that he could look at her. He had forgotten how much shorter she was without her high heels. The familiar scent of her hair engulfed him, and without thinking he bent to kiss her, taking her in his arms. They kissed feverishly, her body clinging to his. She reached up, furrowing his hair with her slender fingers, and drew his face down to hers.

He began kissing her, ears holding her even tighter. She arched her head back so that she could feel the moist warmth of his mouth on her neck. She could feel the heat of his rising passion through the soft fabric of the robe. She reached down to him and he pushed the robe off her shoulders, baring her breasts. He cupped her breast in one hand, brushing her nipple with his thumb, and drew her back to him again, kissing her full on the mouth now, his tongue probing hers.

She pushed him away slightly, breaking their embrace. She looked up at him, the unabashed passion lighting her eyes. Without breaking her gaze, she undid the clasp of her robe, letting it fall where she stood, and began to undo the buttons of his shirt. She kissed his hairless chest and nipples as she progressed downward. She unzipped him and then, watching his eyes, she slipped both hands into his briefs and pushed them down.

Only when he was free of his clothing did she break eye contact and look down at him. She sat down on the sofa in facing him, drawing him to her.

An hour later, they lay satiated in her bed, basking in the afterglow of their passion.

"Why?" he asked quietly.

"Because I wanted you, and I don't really expect to see you or my husband again." Her eyes were sad now.

"Do you think your husband would approve?" Hollingsworth was being flippant, but she took him seriously. She propped herself up on one elbow and looked him in the eyes.
The passion was gone now, replaced with the tenderness he had seen before.

"You make it very hard for me Andrew. I love my husband a great deal and we have an idyllic life together. You know him. You know he is a wonderful man. He loves me too, and we are more in tune mentally and physically than you can ever imagine."

"Ah, that's why you are in bed with me eh?" Hollingsworth's tone amplified the sarcasm.

"No, not at all, it's very hard for me to separate the physical from the emotional. That's why I am so attracted to you, Andrew. Your emotions pour out of you when you make physical love to me. I need that, and frankly you are the only man I have had in my life who has been able to give me that. But I love Michel and I don't believe that I should throw away all that we have had, just because he temporarily succumbed to lust with that tramp."

"Is that all that happened between us? You just succumbed to lust?" The sarcasm was back in his voice.

"No" she replied gently, the tenderness back in her eyes. "If that had been all, we could easily have had a fling and both been on our way. But I was falling in love with you, Andrew. That's why I left. You were too dangerous for me. I knew that there was no way I would ever pick up the pieces with Michel if I let that happen." She paused, touching his face tenderly.

"I'm sorry, I just wanted to try to make it work with Michel. Falling in love with you would have made that impossible." She took her beautifully manicured hand from his face, her eyes still soft.

"I know you don't have anybody else in your life. You weren't giving up one person for another. To be with you, I had to leave somebody I had been happy with for a long time. Besides, you haven't known me long enough for you to know if you are really in love with me. I wanted it to stop before either of us got hurt."

"Well it sure as hell hurt me, I can tell you that!"

"I know, and I'm truly sorry," she said quietly.

They slept until his watch started to vibrate at 2:15 a.m. He dressed quickly, found his nylon bag and slipped quietly out the front door without waking her. He stood for several minutes, watching the stars in a clear black sky, until the car came.

Fik

When Hollingsworth got to the base, the long slender glider trailer was still being loaded onto the cavernous belly of the C130. Lieutenant Ephron was waiting for him.

"Hello again,Mr. Hollingsworth. I have everything here that you asked for. Do you want to look over it all before we leave?

"Good morning, Lieutenant, Did you get the low-altitude charts?"

"Better. I got you 1;4000 topological maps, originally made by Uncle Sam for the Gulf War. They've been updated within the last six months." Ephron grinned.

"Gas? Oil, fuel?"

"I mixed it personally per the engine manual for ASH35, sir. Twenty-five gallons in 5-gallon cans."

"Did somebody fill the oxygen tank in the glider?"

Hollingsworth went through every item that he had written on the checklist the day before. He had made long flights like this many times before. He knew the checklist by heart. But that was in peacetime. This time the stakes were going to be a bit higher than a trophy for a US national speed record.

Hollingsworth was surprised at how quickly the C130 took off. Virtually un-laden, the huge transport aircraft was off the ground in a few hundred feet. The landing gear came up immediately with a loud thud, amplified in the cavernous fuselage where he and Lt Ephron sat on long benches normally occupied by paratroopers. The metal floor had shackles embedded in it every two or three feet. He guessed that these were there to hold down a tank or an armored personnel carrier that he knew the C130 was designed to carry. The glider trailer which was 45 ft long, five feet wide and weighed only 2500 lbs. with the glider in it, was completely dwarfed by its surroundings.

"Bet it doesn't get airborne quite so fast with a tank in here" Hollingsworth yelled at the lieutenant over the horrendous noise of the four turboprop engines.

Ephron smiled at him, unable to hear him from across the wide reverberating fuselage. After a while, the aircraft leveled off as the power was reduced. The vibration which seemed to have permeated Hollingsworth's entire body suddenly stopped, leaving a strange tingling sensation. A crew member came back with two Styrofoam cups of steaming coffee. He spoke in Hebrew to Ephron.

Ephron shouted over to Hollingsworth

"He thinks you are a raving lunatic to try this but he wishes he could come with you."

Hollingsworth raised his cup to the man as he made his way back to the flight deck. They exchanged knowing smiles.

It was too difficult to make conversation over the noise, and Hollingsworth was tired, so he stretched out on the long bench, cinching one of the seat belts around his waist, his bag under his head. In minutes the steady drone of the big turbines lulled him to sleep.

In what seemed like minutes but was, in fact over two hours later, Hollingsworth was awakened by the young Israeli Lieutenant.

"Wake up, sir. We'll be landing in 10 minutes"

Hollingsworth could already sense from the increased pressure in his ears that the aircraft was in a steep descent. He yawned widely to clear his ears. He undid his seat belt and stood up to take a look out of one of the two small windows. It was black outside, almost totally black. As his eyes adjusted, he could just make out the slightly blacker outline of the mountains off to the left. There were only two or three small pinpricks of light on the ground to indicate, any sign of life.

The plane entered a smooth but steep bank and Hollingsworth quickly returned to his seat and fastened the belt. A loud whirring noise like a powerful electric drill started somewhere above his head. "Flaps," he thought to himself.

The crew turned off the interior lights and Hollingsworth could see nothing. He mentally followed the whole landing process in his head. He listened to the mechanical noises and felt the plane bank and pitch under his seat. He heard the landing gear go down and a small red light began to blink above the flight deck door. He felt the nose pitch up slightly then, after what seemed an eternity, they touched down. The landing gear rumbled for a second or two then he was thrown forward in his seatbelt. He could smell the smoke from the huge tires and was pitched forward even harder as the four turbines roared in full reverse thrust, straining to bring the behemoth to a stop.

They were down. The noise stopped except for the engines whining as they wound down. The lights came on.

"Long periods of boredom followed by moments of sheer terror," Ephron quoted an age-old aviation adage. Hollingsworth laughed, and the tension of the landing evaporated.

The Wilga tow plane was parked on the concrete apron, looking like an aluminum praying mantis. It was a highly functional but extremely ugly single-engine light plane. Hollingsworth strode over to meet the stocky pilot.

"I am amazed they got that sucker in here" said the pilot with a noticeable Southern drawl. "Goddam runway is only 2200 feet long. That's if you can call it a runway."

"You're an American," grinned Hollingsworth. "How in hell did they ever find you in the middle of Turkey?" Hollingsworth held out his hand, grinning a sincere greeting. "I'm Andrew Hollingsworth"

"Joe Hensley" said the pilot, shaking his hand. "I ferry these pieces of Polish pot-metal all over the world. I've made two trips to the States in them, up through Scotland, Greenland, Iceland and over to Nova Scotia. They're getting popular with farmers in the Midwest and in Oz. I think the farmers like 'em 'cos they're built like fuckin' tractors." He pounded a fist on the engine cowling to emphasize his point.

"I just brought this one into Turkey two days ago and was hanging around waiting for a ride back on a Polish air-freighter. They called me and asked if I wanted to do a gig as a tow-pilot. I couldn't resist, I had to meet whoever the sonofabitch was who'd be dumb enough to try this stunt. Are you guys making a movie?"

"Have you done much aero-towing?" asked Hollingsworth, ignoring the small talk.

"I bummed around Black Forest glider port in Colorado for a while, I worked at Calistoga before they closed it, and then at Williams. I done a lot of the National contests in the USA. I have about 1500 hours towin', altogether probably over 5000 tows. I haven't done much lately and I ain't never ever towed nobody over the damn mountains at night afore. He was grinning at Hollingsworth now, putting on the Good-Ol' Southern Boy accent as thick as he knew how.

"Did you get a tow hook put on this thing?" Hollingsworth ignored the accent, wondering if the guy was auditioning for a part in the movie.

"I sho' did. I worked all night fabricatin' it mahself. It's a masterpiece even tho' I say it mahself."

Hollingsworth walked around the tail of the plane and knelt down to look at the new tail hook. It was a very professional job.

"Nice job! Thanks."

Hensley got a good look at Hollingsworth when he stood up.

"Ain't you that Brit who flew the 1500 kilometer record down in Oz last year? Hundred and thirty miles an hour or sumpin' like that."

"The very same!". said Hollingsworth "and we weren't makin' no movie then neither." He mimicked Hensley's accent and his double-negative sentence structure, and they both laughed. Mutual respect was established and they began preparation in earnest.

Hollingsworth explained to Hensley what he planned to do. He felt he could trust the man whose life he would depend upon for the next hour, to keep a few little secrets. Joe had heard about the Israelis routing the Islamic fighters but had no idea that it had been Hollingsworth who had made it possible. He knew that if anybody could complete this glider flight, it would be Hollingsworth.

The two talked about the performance of the Wilga when towing a heavy glider. What speed gave the least fuel burn. They needed to leave just enough fuel in the tow plane for it to get back. Not a liter more. How high did Joe think it would climb? Meanwhile Ephron supervised the reassembly of the motor glider. By 05:30, exactly on schedule, they were ready to launch.

and the tow-release in the nose of the glider. He turned on the battery power in the cockpit and flicked a small switch on the joy stick. An electric motor inside the fuselage started up and two bomb-bay-like doors on the top of the fuselage opened up to reveal the bright yellow plastic propeller stowed lengthwise behind the cockpit. The entire engine and prop, mounted on a short pylon pivoted upward and stopped so that the propeller faced forward. The tip of the blade of the propeller barely cleared the top of the rear canopy cover.

Hollingsworth gave the lieutenant instructions about the launch while struggling into his parachute. After a final check that the four cans of fuel were securely fastened in the rear seat, he eased himself into the reclining front seat of the glider. The notoriously temperamental two-stroke engine started fairly easily. Hollingsworth allowed the engine to warm up for a few minutes and then ran it up to full power. Ephron and the tow pilot held the wing tips of the glider and one of the C130 crew held the tail down to prevent the glider from moving. Hollingsworth shut down the power, and after positioning the prop straight up and down, retracted the engine and propeller into the fuselage. The engine-bay doors closed automatically. It was time.

Joe came over to the Glider and handed Hollingsworth a round rubber plug on a chain.

"What's this?" asked Hollingsworth

"What's it look like?" asked Joe with a huge grin. "It's a sink stopper! Figured you might need it."

They both laughed at the joke, understood only by real glider pilots. Joe strolled over to the Wilga, dropping his cigarette and crushing it under the toe of his cowboy boot. He watched Ephron hook up the tow-line to the tail and got in. The Wilga rose off the ground quickly in the cold predawn air. The only sound in the glider was the low hiss from the air vent in the front of the cockpit. They made a long shallow turn toward the mountains. Only the wing-tip lights of the tow-plane were visible against the blackness. They droned onward, climbing steadily until they eventually reached the peaks of the mountains. The altimeter in the glider showed 3000 meters, a little higher than expected thanks to Joe's skillful handling of the Wilga. Hollingsworth put on his cannula and turned on the oxygen flow.

When they reached the Mardin Deglari range, 50 km North of the Turkish-Iranian border, they turned left, heading along the ridge of mountains parallel to the Iranian border. The Wilga would be visible on Iran's defense radar now, but they were still in Turkish territory and it was unlikely that the Iranians would investigate a light aircraft flying outside their airspace even if it was a bit unusual.

As they neared the end of the range, the Wilga's rate of ascent began to decrease in the thin air. The turbocharger was at maximum boost and they would have to level off. They reached 4500 meters (nearly 15,000 feet), a bit short of the 16,000 they had hoped for. Joe didn't have any oxygen in the Wilga and was already beginning to feel a bit slow mentally. Inside the glider it was cold, and Hollingsworth's breath was freezing on the inside of the canopy. He could barely see the tow-plane anymore. He reached for the radio mic and remembered that they had to maintain radio silence. He swung the nose of the glider to the left and then to the right, the signal that he and Joe had agreed to during the ground briefing.

Hollingsworth pulled the release and the Wilga banked away to the left, diving for thicker air.

"Thank God for that!" Joe muttered to himself and added "Good Luck!"

The towline fell away as Hollingsworth turned toward the Iranian border. The Wilga headed directly for the airstrip from which they had departed. He hoped that the radar operators would be distracted by the receding blip from the tow-plane and not notice the very faint echo from the sailplane. Hopefully there was no echo at all. Hollingsworth put the nose down slightly to bring the air speed up to 130 kph, the speed at which he would cover the most ground for the altitude lost.

He turned on the GPS located on the instrument panel. Within a few seconds it displayed his position on a moving map, which showed the terrain and roads around him. It also showed his altitude ,computed from the satellite data. It was within 100 ft of the indication on his altimeter. He made a slight adjustment to his heading to correct for the wind and bring his ground-track in line with the course-line on the screen.

.

The small airplane symbol stayed in the center of the screen and the map moved under it as the glider made progress across the ground. Around the airplane symbol on the screen, an amoeba shape showed how far the glider would travel before reaching 1000' above the terrain. This was calculated from the current rate of descent of the glider, the speed over the ground and the elevation of the terrain. The elevation data came from the map and the other data came from the satellites. The speed over the ground depended on the strength and direction of the wind.

It was an hour before the glider descended to within 1000' of the terrain. He had released the tow-rope at 15,000 feet above mean sea level and he was now at 2000' MSL. He had descended 13,000 ft in 60 minutes and covered a distance of 130 kilometers - six kilometers for every thousand feet of altitude lost.

"Not bad for 15-year-old glider," he thought to himself. He pushed the button on the stick and the engine slowly extended from the bay behind him. He turned on the fuel valve and released the brake holding the propeller, which began wind milling in the airflow. He had to move the trim tab all the way forward in order to maintain the recommended airspeed and compensate for the drag of the propeller. He pulled the choke lever out part way and turned on the ignition. The engine screamed to life like an errant lawn mower, pushing the nose of the plane down. Hollingsworth pulled the trim back quickly and pushed the choke in all the way. He had forgotten how complicated these auxiliary powered sailplanes were to manage under power.

After a few minutes, the engine warmed up and Hollingsworth got the plane trimmed to fly at 85 kph, the speed at which it achieved the best climb-angle. The Vertical Speed Indicator showed 950 ft per minute. Twenty minutes later he reached 16,500 ft, at which the climb rate deteriorated to about 100 ft per minute. He had burned less than 2 gals of gas. He shut off the fuel and turned off the ignition as the engine started to starve. The propeller wind milled again and he quickly trimmed the nose down to compensate for the drag. He waited the requisite 2 minutes to allow the engine exhaust pipe to cool down before retracting it into the flammable fiberglass fuselage.

He watched the propeller in the small mirror in front of him and applied the propeller brake, eventually stopping the propeller in the vertical position so that he could retract the engine. A green light on the panel came on, and he pressed the retract button. The motor whirred for a while and the engine folded down into the rear bay with a satisfying thud. Three green lights came on indicating that the engine was fully retracted and the bay doors closed. Dawn was just breaking over the mountains, the cloudless sky beginning to glow a pale orange.

Hollingsworth repeated this entire process four more times. The sun was higher in the sky and the barren desert had begun to warm. He hit his first thermal at 10:30 am and climbed an easy 5000', circling lazily in the rising air like a buzzard. He headed out on course again, finding each thermal a little bit stronger and higher. He had Koudechah's last position marked on his chart and he now began to estimate where he would be by the time he got to that area. He would have to find Koudechah from the air. He could not use the radio to contact him without giving away his position to the Arabs. They would be able to get to him in less than half an hour.

Koudechah wouldn't see or hear the glider unless he was within a half mile. He decided that the best approach would be to use the engine so that Koudechah would hear him coming. He would fly a low search pattern centered on his estimated position. He would have to find a place to land first then, once Koudechah had been found and he saw the glider, Hollingsworth would fly off in the direction of the landing site. Hopefully, Koudechah would understand and follow on foot. Hollingsworth studied the area on the chart, intently trying to visualize the terrain. It was pretty rough and there wouldn't be a lot of places to land a glider with a 26.5 meter (87') wingspan.

The thermal he was in was strong, and he worked it until it began to weaken at 16,000'. He guessed he would not need the engine again until he got to Koudechah. There was a distinctive row of rocky outcrops in the area where he expected to find him. He circled them on his chart and entered their latitude and longitude into his GPS. He was flying between thermals at 200 kph now, and would just pull up in the weaker thermals rather than spend time circling. He was racing against the sun now. He still had plenty of gas left but he wanted to reserve that for the search.

His GPS began to beep at about the same time as he spotted the three rocky outcrops in a perfect straight line. They stood out in the otherwise featureless desert. Only the dry "wadi" creeks and the occasional patch of pale green marsh marked the few areas where any water reached the surface. He turned parallel to the line of rocks and started looking for a reasonable place to land. The charts he had obtained from Ephron showed a road that ran along his course- line, but he could see no sign of it from 2500' above the ground. He made a graceful 180-degree turn and flew back along the rocks in the opposite direction. For the first time he started to have doubts that he would find Koudechah in this vast desert.

The terrain was strewn with rocks and dry vegetation that, from the air, looked like sagebrush.. He noticed a short area where there were no rocks. It looked as if the sand had been bulldozed, leaving a flat area devoid of rocks. He doubled back and could now see that it was a disused road. Sand had blown over the road, leaving only short stretches where it was visible at all. He decided that he would be able to land the glider there if the engine failed to start. He trimmed the glider to 85 kph, deployed the engine, and descended to about a thousand feet above the road. He flew up and down the road. trying to assess the condition. The sand had drifted across the road in several places and looked as if it was very deep. There were two or three stretches of road that were clear, but the surface didn't look good. Deep gullies crossed the road in several placed, no doubt eroded by heavy seasonal rain and flood waters.

He turned to make another pass in the opposite direction and thought he saw something out of the corner of his eye. He pushed the stick hard over and carved a tight turn. The long wings curved gracefully under the 3g stress. The blazing sun was now glinting off the rocks, and he lost sight of the object that had caught his eye. He levelled the wings and flew parallel to the road.

He recognized the tattered flight suit first. It was Koudechah. He had scrambled out from behind some rocks and was now in the middle of the road waving both his arms in the air like a desperate scarecrow. He stopped to aim a small signaling mirror in the direction of the glider. Hollingsworth pushed the nose down and flew past him at 100' above the ground, less than 50 yards away. He was so close that Koudechah recognized his face.

"Jesus Christ, this is my lucky day," Hollingsworth said out loud to himself. He pulled the glider up and, banking over, gave Koudechah a nonchalant salute. He couldn't believe he had found him so easily. It was incredible.

Hollingsworth climbed back to 1000 feet and put the engine away. It was much easier and safer to land the glider with the engine retracted. He put the landing gear down and brought in 10 degrees of flap. He glided downwind to the lower end of the road and turned 90 degrees toward the road, judging his altitude and looking at the deep mounds of sand across the road. He turned final and added another 10 degrees of flap. The road looked really rough and a deep gully ran across it just about where he expected to touch down.

"Oh shit!" he exclaimed, realizing that he might touch down just before the gully. "That will tear the landing gear off. He was now a few feet of the ground doing 80 kph.

"Fuck it!" he said aloud, "I'm gonna put this mother down with the wheel up". At the last second, just 50 feet above the ground, Hollingsworth pulled the gear retract lever and added a full landing flaps. He was skimming the surface only a few inches above the ground, the wings slicing through the air like two long scythes. He kept easing the stick back, holding the plane off the ground. He passed over the fissure in the roadway and let the plane settle onto the soft sandy surface.

The noise of the pristine white belly of the glider grinding over the sand was sickening. It seemed to go on forever, but in fact the 1500-pound plane stopped dead in less than the length of a football field. Hollingsworth opened the canopy. He was drenched in sweat.

He got out of the plane and took a long drink from his water bottle. The plane was buried about six inches in the sand. He couldn't tell if there was any damage other than to the gel-coat and paint. He walked up the road another 20 yards or so. Another gaping fissure was ahead about 4 feet across and at least 2 ft deep. If he had hit that with the wheel down it would have torn out the landing gear when it hit the other side of the gully. It had been a good last-minute decision, but he wondered if he should have spent more time looking for a better place to land.

"No," he said to himself "I would have used too much fuel. "

Koudechah was running up the road and leapt the gully almost into Hollingsworth's arms. He was unshaven and blistered from the sun. He looked like Humphrey Bogart in the African Queen.

"You crazy, how you say, crazy English fucking mother!" Koudechah had never quite got the hang of swearing in English. "You came to get me!"

They hugged, slapping each other's backs, jumping up and down like two teenagers whose team had just won the big game. They had started walking back toward the plane when Koudechah stopped in his tracks.

"Oh No!" he said "you are forgetting the wheels to put down. We are finish, Kaput. Merde! How you be so stupid!" Hollingsworth couldn't help laughing at the mixture of French and German all put together, no doubt, with Hebrew syntax.

"Why you laugh?" demanded Koudechah "Not funny this. Now both in deep shit."

"I landed with the wheel retracted deliberately Michel. If I had gone into one of these gullies it would have torn the landing gear right off the plane. I don't think there is any serious damage, but I can't tell. If you help me lift the tail up high in the air, I'll put the wheel down and we can take a look."

"You make this stupid mistake on purpose?" Koudechah looked confused

"Yes, just give me a hand to lift the tail. Let's get it up on your shoulder then I'll go to the cockpit and put the wheel down. The two men lifted the tail of the glider until it rested on its nose and one wing tip.

"Can you hold it while I drop the gear?"

"Is there alternative?" grunted Michel, holding close to 500 lbs. on his shoulder.

Hollingsworth dropped the gear, and the two men gently lowered the tail down so that the plane now stood on the main wheel and the tail wheel. Hollingsworth lay down in the sand next to the plane and examined the belly of the glider. It was badly scraped and the front corners of the undercarriage doors had been ground off.

"Looks OK to me, but I don't know what the glider club is going to say when they see it. They don't even know we borrowed it!"

Koudechah helped him up.

"How can ever repay you for risking life for me, Andrew?" asked Koudechah, still gripping his hand.

"Oh, come on Michel, you would do the same for me, and we don't have time for that crap right now. If we ever make it back you can get me a ride in one of those new F128's of yours. We first need to figure out how we are going to get back".

Hollingsworth started to think out loud. He had taken off at 0600. It was 1300 now, so it had taken him 7 hours to get here. He had burned 40 of the 58 liters of fuel they could carry, but he had been aero towed off the ground. Going back, he would have to take off and climb using the fuel on board. The thermals that had helped him get here would probably die after 1800 hrs and he would have to use the engine for 5 hours at least. It was going to be very tight.

"We need to get out of here ASAP, Michel. Get those gas cans out of the back seat and don't spill any - we don't have enough as it is."

Koudechah undid the seat belts and shoulder harness holding the cans in place on the rear seat, then passed the cans Hollingsworth

"There's a funnel and some tubing in the back there, too"

Koudechah held the funnel while Hollingsworth poured the precious fuel. They were already working as the team they had been before, each anticipating the actions of the other and moving to assist, without the need for words or direction.

"We'll need to push it back as far as we can to take off. I'm not sure there is enough road between these two gullies to get off the ground. This soft sand is going to really slow us down."

"What is the takeoff distance?" asked Koudechah nonchalantly

"Seven hundred and fifty feet on a smooth hard surface, at sea level, on a standard day. It's hot here and we are 2000' above sea level so I'd guess its nearer to 1000"

"Merde!" said Koudechah, looking back down the road, gauging the distance to the first gully that Hollingsworth had flown over. "Merde!" he repeated.

"Well" said Hollingsworth, "let's push it down there and get ready. The Queen's own Royal Engineers ain't about to come out here and build us a new runway. So unless you plan on walking back to Tel Aviv, let's move it! Koudechah looked at him quizzically, and they started pushing the glider through the soft sand. They were both sweating profusely by the time they had pushed it back to the gully.

"I'm not sure we'll get off the ground unless we remove some of this sand where it is really deep. If we get bogged down in the sand it's all over. I have to have enough airspeed to balloon up over that gap up there. Understand?" Hollingsworth gestured up the road from where they dragged the glider.

"Let's take the seat pans out and use them as shovels" suggested Koudechah "I take out, you shovel!" they both laughed. They got a screwdriver from the tool kit and began removing the molded fiberglass seat pans from the plane. They shoveled away the patches of deeper sand, and after an hour they had a wavy two-foot-wide swath of clear concrete down the middle of the road. Both men were sweating and exhausted.

"You bring any beer?" asked Koudechah rummaging in the small baggage area behind the rear cockpit.

"Who do you think this is - Pan American?" Hollingsworth retorted, tossing the seat pans back in the glider.

"They kaput!" cried Koudechah, throwing up his hands and laughing again.

"Yes, and we'll be kaput too if we don't get to hell out of here. Put that seat pan back in, get your 'chute on, and get in.

"No need 'chutes," said Koudechah "No chute, less weight, right? We fly off ground, sooner right?

"Yes, I agree skip the chutes". Hollingsworth could think of other reasons they might need the 'chutes, but kept them to himself.

"I found bunch of scrolls in a cave I hid in when the helicopters were overhead. I brought one. Ok?"

"Oh, for God's sake, yes, now get in." Hollingsworth was getting impatient.

Hollingsworth extended the engine and checked that everything was ok after the gear-up landing, and got in the front seat. He went meticulously through the preflight checklist and pressed the starter. The engine cranked over four or five times but it failed to start. He waited a few seconds and tried again with the same result.

"Shit, don't get bloody temperamental now!" he muttered to himself From the back seat, Koudechah yelled "She flooded! I smelling the gas." He was an old hand with two stroke dirt bikes.

Hollingsworth knew what to do. He pushed the throttle in all the way with his left hand, and with the fuel-valve off, pushed the starter again. The engine roared to life at full throttle, taking him by surprise. He quickly adjusted the throttle, and the plane started moving down the road. It was difficult to steer with one wingtip dragging in the sand, but he got it centered in the path they had made all the way down the road. The wing lifted up and he got the tail off the ground so he could steer with the rudder. The gully across their improvised runway was coming up fast.

At the last-minute Hollingsworth moved the flap handle to 15 degrees and the glider ballooned up a foot or two in the air. It seemed like an eternity before it bounced gently on the other side of the gaping crevasse in the road. They were just about airborne again with the wheel just a few inches from the ground. Hollingsworth then took a horrendous risk.

"It's now or never," he exclaimed and retracted the gear. With a little less drag and another foot of ground-clearance the plane began to accelerate. They were well and truly airborne.

"We making it!" exclaimed Koudechah from the rear cockpit. "By God we fucking making it! You are shiny Professor!"

"You mean brilliant, right?" Hollingsworth asked, chuckling to himself at Koudechah's English

"Yes, you fucking brilliant flying!" They both relaxed a little bit and began the climb out.

Hollingsworth found a good thermal and worked it up to 3000 feet with the engine running. He levelled off, put the engine away, and rejoined the same thermal. In less than thirty minutes they were at 14,000 feet, and Hollingsworth turned on course.

They made good time, averaging 160 kph until the sun started to get low in the sky and the thermals got weaker and further apart. Hollingsworth was exhausted. He had been up since 2 am and already flown over 1000 km.

"Think you can fly this for a bit Michel?" Hollingsworth knew what the answer would be.

"Sure, I could fly bus if you put wings on"

"Just stay on this heading and trim it out to 90 knots. No faster. Wake me up if we get below about 3000 ft AGL."

About 30 minutes later, Hollingsworth was awakened by the Variometer beeping rapidly. They had run into another booming thermal. Hollingsworth took the controls and banked the glider over into the thermal which took them back to 16,000 ft altitude in less than 20 minutes. This happened about every 30 to 45 minutes. They climbed rapidly, then Koudechah would glide to the next good thermal while Hollingsworth napped. Several hours later, they could see the mountains over a hundred miles away. As the afternoon wore on and the sun got lower in the sky, the thermals got weaker and topped out lower. Hollingsworth started to slow down between the thermals, cruising at 120 knots instead of 140. He figured that he would get to the Mountains before the sun went down.

Hollingsworth climbed slowly in a soft thermal and had to work hard to reach 10,000 ft altitude. The sun was very low in the sky and the lift was dying. At 3000 feet above the desert, Hollingsworth deployed the engine and started it. The noise awakened Koudechah who had dozed off in the back seat.

"What happen?" asked Koudechah nervously.

"I started the engine," Hollingsworth shouted over the scream of the tiny engine. "The sun's going down and the thermals are dying now. The Turkish border is on the other side of those mountains. I think we can get there using the motor and any weak lift we find on the way. We have used fuel only to take off, so we should be able to make it."

The glider droned on at just 60 knots, the best speed to make the most distance with the fuel they had left. Any faster and they would consume more fuel and descend faster. Just as the sun disappeared over the mountains, a Russian MIG appeared off their right wingtip. Neither of them had heard it over the noise of the glider engine. The MIG couldn't fly as slowly as the glider so it passed them quite quickly with the nose held high, flaps down and gear extended. They could see the pilot gesturing them to land. They ignored him.

The MIG came around a second time. This time, the pilot had deployed the dive brakes to slow the jet down. But it was still going 25 knots faster than the glider. It turned away to make another pass.

"Can we go slower?" ask Koudechah

"Sure." Said Hollingsworth, bringing the nose of the glider up until the airspeed indicator showed 50 knots. The MIG came around again on the left side of the glider, and Koudechah noticed the MIG nose pitch up very slightly in a vain attempt to slow the jet down even more. Koudechah took the stick, and as the MIG came alongside he turned violently toward the Russian fighter. Hollingsworth gasped.

The MIG pilot reacted as Koudechah had expected, and used full aileron deflection to try to turn the jet away and avoid a certain collision. But the MIG was already at minimum airspeed and barely controllable. It rolled over instantly and went into a violent spin, barely missing the glider. It was too low to recover from the spin, and the fighter hit the ground and exploded in a ball of flame. It happened too quickly for the pilot to bail out.

Hollingsworth took the controls and turned the glider back on their original heading, and they droned on for a few minutes. Neither of the two men spoke.

"They are NOT going to believe it when we tell them you downed a MIG, Colonel! Tell me, what were you going to do if he hadn't tried to turn away?" asked Hollingsworth

"Ram him!" replied Koudechah casually. "What did we have to lose?"

They made it to the Mountains where Hollingsworth found a low "saddle" through which he threaded the glider, now flying only a few hundred feet above the steep terrain. He soared along the mountains in the dusk, using the wind rising up the slope to maintain altitude. Once he had the Fik airport in site, Hollingsworth stowed the engine and began a final glide.

Call them on the radio Colonel. Tell them we'll be there in ten minutes and to put the coffee on."

They landed just as the sun set. They were barely able to get out of the glider; which Hollingsworth had flown 1800 miles in two days. The back of his flight suit was wet from perspiration, and he realized that he had peed himself when the Colonel had tried to ram the MIG. He owed Koudechah his life. Standing next to the glider, Hollingsworth reached out to shake the Colonel's hand but, instead, Koudechah grasped the professor in a bone-crushing bear hug. Then, standing back, he shook Hollingsworth's hand in both of his. The Colonel was near to tears.

"How can I thank you enough, Prof. You risked your life to come get me."

Hollingsworth contemplated saying "you could stop beating your wife," but thought better of it. He turned, patting the glider affectionately on the nose.

"Thank you, Iris." he said under his breath, "Thank you for being my guardian angel."

Ephron, the young lieutenant who had accompanied them on the cargo flight into Fik, interrupted them. He saluted Koudechah crisply, and hurriedly congratulated them both.

"Sorry to interrupt sir, but we have an aircraft waiting for Mr. Hollingsworth." He motioned Hollingsworth toward the Gulfstream jet that was waiting on the ramp.

"Sorry, Mr. Hollingsworth, no SR72 to take you home. This is Mr. Gibli's personal aircraft. It will take us to Mashabim, where a US Airforce transport plane is waiting to take you home to the USA."

Hollingsworth had to think about that. "Home" had been the UK, but he had lived in the US for over a year now. He liked the weather much more than the cold drizzle of England, and he loved the people he worked with and worked for. An entrepreneurial "can-do" attitude pervaded most of the Americans he had met. They also had sense of real freedom that didn't exist in England any more. The "UK nanny state" provided all and controlled all. That was not the way Hollingsworth wanted to live his life.

"Yes!" said Hollingsworth emphatically. "let's go home."

They boarded the Gulfstream jet, which took off almost immediately. The plane was sumptuously outfitted. The rear of the aircraft contained a bedroom with a queen-sized bed, and a full bathroom, complete with climate-controlled shower, commode and bidet.

The center of the aircraft contained an office and a wall of high-tech communications hardware including satellite links. The front of the aircraft, where they sat, was set up as a lounge, with comfortable reclining chairs with side tables and built-in telephones.

The young lieutenant went to the compact galley and poured coffee for Hollingsworth and himself. Settling in the chair across from Hollingsworth, he said apologetically,

"Mr. Gibli sends his regrets that he wasn't able to meet you personally today. The Arab defenses have been decimated, thanks largely to you, and they want to negotiate a 'lasting' peace."

The lieutenant sneered as he uttered the word 'lasting'. Hollingsworth chuckled. "Peace until they get better electronics, eh?" Hollingsworth laughed. "If they only knew what they were really up against they would never have tried to invade Israel, would they, Ephron?"

The young lieutenant looked perplexed, and Hollingsworth realized that he wasn't aware of Israel's devastating nuclear defenses which would have been unleashed if the invasion had succeeded.

"Why the rush to get me out of Israel?" asked Hollingsworth, wondering if the young man would know the answer to his question. The young Lieutenant answered very simply.

"The Prime Minister believes that the US Congress might construe your activity in Israel as Military Aid. Aid that was not sanctioned by Congress. The fact that this was a private transaction between two international companies is irrelevant to the Left-Wing Socialists who seem to have gained complete control of the Democrat Party. The Democrats would classify unsanctioned aid as another impeachable offense by the Republicans and tar all the conservative candidates with the same brush. The election of a new president is only weeks away. He personally hopes that Trump's protégé gets elected and that she continues with policies that are favorable to Israel. In the meantime, he thinks it is wise to keep America's activity in Israel a secret until after the election."

Hollingsworth acknowledged the response with a nod and lay back in the reclining seat. Sometime later, Lt. Ephron woke him up.

"We have a minor change in plan Mr. Hollingsworth. We now have clearance to fly you direct to Ramstein Air Base in Germany. A different aircraft is taking you home. We will be landing there in about 90 minutes. Use the bed in the rear cabin if you would like to take a nap, sir."

Hollingsworth took up the offer and retired to the rear cabin. He had no sooner laid down on the comfortable double bed than he fell into a fitful sleep. He woke himself up several times, his limbs twitching as he relived the interception by the MIG in his mind. He would consciously tell himself again, that they had nothing to lose, and go back to sleep.

The Co-Pilot, wearing civilian airline uniform, came into the rear cabin and woke him up.

"We are about 20 minutes from the US Airbase at Ramstein, sir. The pilot asks if you would like to join him in the cockpit."

"I would, I would. Give me a couple of minutes," Hollingsworth replied, a little bit groggy from his fitful sleep. He went into the tiny bathroom connected to the bedroom and slapped a little cold water onto his face. He peered at his own face in the mirror. He somehow looked older.

He made his way to the cockpit, refusing the cup of coffee proffered by the Lieutenant. The pilot motioned Hollingsworth to sit in the right seat, which the co-Pilot had vacated.

"Ever flown a Gulfstream?" he asked.

"No, I'm a glider pilot. I have flown a few jets on simulators, that's about it" Hollingsworth replied humbly

"Are you the guy that just fetched Colonel Koudechah out of the desert in that glider we just saw back there?" the pilot asked, with a knowing look on his face.

"What glider?" replied Hollingsworth in a tone that abruptly extinguished the Pilot's curiosity.

"Your Airplane," said the pilot turning over the controls to Hollingsworth, "don't break anything."

Hollingsworth took the controls for a short while. The aircraft was like driving a Mack truck after the Ferrari performance of the F16D. The two men talked about the features of the Gulfstream, which the pilot was very proud to demonstrate. After a few minutes the radio came alive with Air Traffic control announcements, and the pilot motioned the co-pilot to regain his seat. The Pilot shook hands with Hollingsworth and said warmly,

"An honor to meet you sir. Have a good trip home."

Hollingsworth went back to his seat in the lounge cabin.

"I'll have that cup of coffee now Lieutenant, if we have time before we land."

The inevitable black Chevy Tahoe met the plane on the apron, and Ephron lowered the gangway. He took Hollingsworth's passport from his pocket and, after checking every page, returned it to Hollingsworth.

"Colonel Koudechah asked me to make sure you got this," said the Lieutenant, handing him the sink stopper that they had carried in the glider. "He said to tell you that it worked!"

Hollingsworth laughed, and they shook hands vigorously and sincerely. The driver of the Tahoe took Hollingsworth's bag and opened the rear door for him. They drove off in silence. Ephron gave him a crisp salute as the car passed by. A few minutes later the car drew up at the back of a huge hangar at the far end of the airport. The driver got out and opened the rear door for Hollingsworth.

"Through that door, sir!" the driver pointed to a small personnel-door in the huge corrugated steel wall. Hollingsworth tried the hangar door but it appeared to be locked. He rapped twice with his free hand. The door was opened by an attractive woman who Hollingsworth recognized immediately as Nikki Haley, the US ambassador to the United Nations until 2019 and now the Republican nominee for POTUS.

"Mr. Hollingsworth?" she asked, extending her hand cordially. "We've been expecting you. Come on in."

Hollingsworth entered the cavernous hangar, in which was parked a US Airforce Boeing C-32, a highly modified 757. Haley introduced Hollingsworth to Condoleezza Rice, Haley's popular pick for Secretary of State, and Patrick Shanahan, the incumbent Secretary of Defense.

Hollingsworth was way over his head. He had rubbed shoulders with high-ranking military leaders from all over the world. That was part of his job in the Electronic Warfare Industry. But he didn't like politicians much, and tried to avoid them.

A man in Airforce uniform appeared. He introduced himself to Hollingsworth.

"Hello, I am Lt. Col. Stack. Welcome aboard Airforce II. 'll be your pilot today." He turned to the others and said "Ladies and Gentlemen, we have an immediate clearance for departure. If you would all re-board the aircraft, we will get underway. Mr. Hollingsworth, feel free to join us on the flight-deck after we turn off the seatbelt sign."

The main hangar doors began to open, and the group boarded the aircraft via a roll-up gangway. Nikki Haley turned to Hollingsworth and said, laughing, "how come you get the special treatment? I want to sit in the cockpit too!"

The Boeing 757 spartan compared to Gibli's Gulfstream. The seats in the front cabin were like first class seats in an airline, with four rows of two comfortable reclining seats on each side of the aisle. A bulkhead with a closed door separated the front section from the rest of the aircraft. Haley took a window seat in the second row and asked Hollingsworth to join her. Hollingsworth stowed his bag in the overhead compartment and sat down beside her.

"We've been in the Middle East as part of a delegation to monitor the peace agreement that the UIA is negotiating with the Israelis. We wanted to make sure that the Arabs know we fully support the Israelis." She paused and looked over at Hollingsworth

"What were you doing in Israel, Mr. Hollingsworth?"

Hollingsworth was tongue tied. There was no record of him being in Israel, and the Israeli Prime Minister had thought it wise that nobody knew he had been there. Yet Haley seemed to know that he had been in Israel and might have been briefed on the "project". or... she was fishing. Hollingsworth didn't know which.

"I wasn't in Israel." He said firmly. Haley raised her eyebrows slightly, and knowingly raised an index finger to the side of her nose and changed the subject. She began to talk about the discussions they had witnessed between the Israelis and the Arabs. Hollingsworth figured that if she knew about the IFF systems, she would give him credit for his discretion; and if she didn't, he would get credit for not revealing the USA's involvement in the conflict. He didn't expect the subject to come up again.

Hollingsworth learned about the huge blow the Israelis had inflicted on all the forces of the Arab coalition. The Syrians had lost most of their aircraft, and their ground defense systems had been complete wiped out. Jordan suffered a similar fate, and the troops and tanks on those two borders were virtually annihilated. The Syrian and Jordan leaders blamed the Iranians for underestimating the strength and capability of the Israeli forces and for failing to provide forward intelligence on the attack. According to Haley, the meeting frequently devolved into the typical Arab tribal chaos. As she put it, "the future of the Arab Alliance didn't look good."

After a short while, Hollingsworth went up to the flight deck. The C-32 pilots were aware that he was a pilot but knew nothing about his exploits in Israel, and he didn't tell them. The crew familiarized him with the aircraft and let him fly the plane for a while. He found it boring and quickly excused himself. He went back to the cabin, where he settled into one of the big recliners and dozed off.

The cabin crew woke him up with a cup of coffee as they made the approach into Andrews Airforce Base. As they disembarked, Haley took Hollingsworth aside, holding him back by his arm.

"I was briefed on your mission in Israel, Andrew, and I want to thank you personally for your contribution. From all accounts, the Israelis, and the entire Middle East owes you a huge debt of gratitude. Oh... and Ms. Batault should be very thankful that she has you for a friend." She squeezed his arm and turned to leave.

"By the way," she added over her shoulder, "we made it clear to the Arabs that if they try that again, the USA will enter the World Oil market and sell our surplus oil below their market price. We will bankrupt the Arab oil producers who support the UIA within three months. We're producing more than enough oil to do that now. You and I will talk more in the future. Good luck to you, Andrew." She hurried off to catch up with the others.

The Airforce put him up in Officer's Quarters for the night, and the next day he left on a commercial flight back to San Francisco, where Jack Husher met him at the airport.

Husher wasn't happy. He took Hollingsworth's bag and angrily laid into him.

"What the hell do you think you were doing, flying that glider into Iran, Andrew? If something had happened to you, this company would be finished. The investors would crucify me for allowing it to happen, and the USA would lose the only guy in the world who knows how to build effective IFF electronics. What in the name of God possessed you to take such a ridiculous risk Andrew?"

"It's a long story Jack." Andrew replied, very subdued.

"I should fire you!" Husher responded angrily, and they drove in silence back to Hollingsworth's apartment.

"Be at the office at seven sharp. We have a lot to do and you will need to catch up!" Then, in a softer voice Husher added.

"Well done, Andrew, an astounding effort against all odds. I can't thank you enough."

Hollingsworth smiled "Not firing me will be enough" he said, and Husher grinned, his eyes softening.

The apartment hadn't been occupied in six months. It felt damp and dreary. Hollingsworth vowed to get a nicer place and make it his home. The next morning, the whole team was assembled in the lab to welcome him home. There were quite a few new people who were introduced enthusiastically. Gordon Hadley, who had been officially appointed CEO by the board of directors, welcomed Hollingsworth personally.

"Good to have you back, Andrew," he said warmly.

The "boys in white lab coats" were eager to tell him about the new developments. They had added another microprocessor that handled the satellite interface. Now the system started all the processes at once, so that as soon as the satellite data had been obtained, the system was ready to go. They showed him the prototype they had built on their own. It looked more like some of roadside IEDs Hollingsworth had seen in Israel rather than a piece of aircraft electronics.

But Hollingsworth praised them all for being innovative and having the guts to experiment to produce a working model, "ugly as it might be,." as he humorously put it.

The crowd dispersed and Hollingworth, Hadley and Husher went into Hadley's office. Husher asked Hadley's secretary to bring some coffee and some fig newtons, "to spur the group's imagination." She didn't get the intimation. Husher started to explain "figments", but gave up.

Hadley led the impromptu meeting.

"Give us a blow-by-blow account Andrew. I can't believe you tested this thing for the first time in a combat role. That must have taken some guts!" Hadley showed genuine admiration for what they had done in Israel.

"We didn't have an option," Hollingsworth retorted humbly.

Hollingsworth went on to explain the intelligence the Israelis had about the troop and tanks amassing on their borders. He told them how they knew that the Iranians had insisted that the invasion should take place on a Holy day, and how this had given the team an extra 24 hours to over-fly Syria and verify that they could hack the satellite quickly enough to arm the IFF system and enable them to look like friendly aircraft.

Husher interjected irately when Hollingsworth told them that he was in the back seat of the F16D on that test-flight.

"Christ, Andrew! Don't you have ANY brains! You could have been killed! That's even worse than that stupid…" Husher stumbled looking for the right words, "that stupid PRANK you pulled with the damn glider!"

"Jack, I was the only person on the planet who knew how to operate the IFF system we had just installed in the F16. What would YOU have done?"

Husher grumbled under his breath and poured himself a glass of water from the carafe on the table. Hollingsworth described the uneventful flight over Syria, but didn't mention the victory-roll over the field with full afterburners. He spent a lot of time talking about all the issues he and Koudechah had while trying to install the system in the F16D, and how they overcame some of the problems, repeating the process in the 50 single-seat fighters. There were a lot of questions raised, and by the time they were finished it was nearly lunch time.

Husher held Hollingsworth back as they group dispersed for lunch.

"Back here at 13:00,." he said to the group, and then to Hollingsworth, "I hear you got a ride on Airforce Two back to Andrews. Tell me about that in private, OK?"

"I will," Hollingsworth replied and picked up a ham sandwich off the buffet on the way back to his 'hovel', as his colleagues called his untidy office. He checked his e-mails on the computer and the text messages on his phone. He always looked for messages from Nicole.

As usual, there were none from her. There was a text from Husher: "dinner at home tonight. Peggy is making meat loaf.". Hollingsworth responded, "Sounds good!" The meeting droned on all afternoon. Team members joined the meeting as needed, and by the time they were done they had a two-page "to-do list" of all the things they needed to accomplish to get the product properly "packaged" and put into production. Some items could be accomplished in a few hours, others would take weeks. The person whose name appeared next to each item had until Friday to confirm the completion date and come up with a plan to make it happen. The process wasn't pretty - but it worked.

At dinner that evening, Peggy welcomed Hollingsworth with open arms. She treated Andrew like a brother, and every time they met, she fussed over his health, well-being, and, lack of female companionship. After the usual greetings she quickly got down to business - her business, that is.

"I hear you met Nikki Haley! What was she like, is she still married to that Liberal twit? Is she as strong-willed as she appears?"

Hollingsworth, laughed, and held up his hand to stop the torrent of questions.

"Yes, I spent some time with her on the plane, she is lovely. She really is just like she is on TV. Very genuine... and yes, she is still married to that Liberal twit. Happily, so, I might add." Hollingsworth laughed at his last remark. He knew Peggy would try to "fix him up" with Nikki if she could. Jack was more interested in the mindset of the woman who was very likely to be the next president of the United States. Trump's second term had been another economic triumph, and another conservative majority in both houses seemed likely. Husher believed that politics drove the Capital Markets in the USA, and wanted to know if his own bets were safe.

Hollingsworth hadn't talked to Nikki Haley about many of these subjects, but told Husher that she had left the door open for him to call her about "anything he needed, and to say hello to Jack." He gave Husher the card that Haley had given him for "safe-keeping". It would soon disappear in his own office.

When he left, Peggy gave him a big hug and whispered in his ear.

"Call Nicole, Andrew."

But he didn't, and time flew by as the team strove to make every item on the "to-do list" happen on time - but rarely under budget. Meanwhile, Hollingsworth found himself a small three-bedroom "cottage" overlooking the sea in Carmel and spent his weekends there, retaining the apartment for convenience. He bought a used Porsche 911 and had it restored to showroom condition. The company did very well, selling the new systems to nearly all the European Military and, of course, to the USA. The Israeli company received over seven million dollars for the 50 devices that were delivered and for installation and training "in the field." As agreed, the Israeli company shared the spoils with its American partner. Husher took the company public and Hollingsworth's shares turned out to be worth three million dollars, despite the dilution that the founders had to accept to get the second round of financing. The risks, both financial and physical, had paid off handsomely. Life was good!

Three months later, Hollingsworth was sitting in his office when his cell phone rang. The screen displayed "NICOLE B." Hollingsworth was surprised, and took a minute to gather his wits before answering.

"Hello," he said very tentatively... not sure what to expect.

"It's Nicole,." she said quietly.

"Yes, I know."

"I am afraid I have some bad news, Andrew." Her voice breaking slightly, she continued: "Michel has been killed in a car accident. I thought you ought to know." She chose the words carefully, not sure that Andrew would want to know but certain he should know. It took Hollingsworth a few seconds to answer.

"I am genuinely sorry to hear that. He was a great guy." Hollingsworth also chose his words carefully. Careful not to say he was a "good" guy, because he knew he wasn't, not to Nicole anyway. There was a subtle difference.

"The funeral is next week. Full military honors. It would be good if you were there. You were a big part of the most important event in his life." There was a short silence on the phone, and Nicole held her breath waiting for Andrew to politely decline.

"I'll be there," he replied firmly.

"Good!" Nicole said, relieved, then added tentatively, "How have you been?"

"Life is good,." he answered, wanting to tell her how much he missed her. "Life is very good. We can talk when I see you next week."

"D'accord," she said, and quietly hung up, sensing that this wasn't the time for a deeper conversation.

Hollingsworth sat for several minutes, holding the mobile phone in his hand, contemplating calling her back. Instead, he went on line and booked a first-class flight to Tel Aviv on the following Wednesday. He left the return flight open. He fleetingly considered a stop at home in London, but reminded himself that HOME was now Carmel, CA. He sent a text to Hadley asking for some time off. He found himself counting the hours until he left for Tel Aviv, but wasn't thinking about Koudechah's funeral. The thought of seeing Nicole again distracted him completely.

The team came up with a casing design for the unit and were anxious for Hollingsworth to approve it before he left, but he wouldn't.

"It's just too damn big, guys!" he told them impatiently. "You need to go and look at the aircraft that we are going to put this thing into and either design a configuration for each one or come up with something that goes on the outside. Trust me! This won't fit!" Hadley was surprised at Hollingsworth's impatience and put it down to the pressure of the job. But it wasn't. Hollingsworth just wanted to get to Tel Aviv.

"OK!" Hadley conceded reluctantly, "We'll get it changed while you're in Israel. Have a safe trip. No gliders, sailplanes, whatever you call them, right?"

Hollingsworth laughed. He was glad that Hadley didn't know about the encounter with the MIG..."

Tel Aviv

He picked up his small bag from customs and joined the long line at immigration. When Hollingsworth got to the front of the line, the officer asked him if he had visited Israel before. Hollingsworth answered absent mindedly that he had.

"When was that, sir?" the officer asked. Hollingsworth realized he had screwed up. The officer was now scrutinizing Hollingsworth's passport looking for evidence of entry into Israel. Hollingsworth began to sweat.

"No sorry, I was supposed to come here about 6 months ago but that trip got cancelled. I travel so much, it's hard to keep track. I haven't visited Israel before. I'm looking forward to it." The officer looked directly into Hollingsworth's eyes, stamped his passport and handed it back to him.

"Welcome to Israel, Mr. Hollingsworth. Enjoy your stay." Hollingsworth had a feeling that he was going to be watched every moment he spent in Israel.

Nicole was waiting for him at the exit to the Customs area. He spotted her trademark red coat immediately, followed by the green eyes. His heart skipped a beat or two.

"Sa va?" they both said at the same time. She kissed him on both cheeks. He felt it more as French formality rather than with any affection.

I got you a hotel room close to where I live. My place is very small, with only one bedroom, otherwise I would ask you to stay."

"You moved from that lovely place?" Hollingsworth asked

"Yes! I left Michel a month after you went back to the States. Something happened to him during that air battle and he started drinking again. He hit me. He knocked me out and left me on the kitchen floor and took off. A neighbor heard the ruckus and called the police, who took me to hospital. I left him as soon as I got out of hospital. That was nearly nine months ago."

"Merde!" said Hollingsworth, slipping into French vernacular. "Why didn't you call me?"

"Ditto" she responded curtly in English, and they drove in an awkward silence for a while. Nicole finally broke the ice.

"Michel told everybody about you rescuing him in that glider, you know. He thought you were the best pilot he had ever met. He claimed that you both downed a MIG but nobody believed him. He left that scroll he found in the desert to you in his, will by the way. He said you were the only person who knew where he found it. He also left some notes for you. He believed they revealed some information about Mohammed that would rock the Muslim World."

"We did down a MIG." Hollingsworth responded in a serious tone. "Michel tried to ram the MIG and the guy took evasive action, which Michel had predicted. But the Russian plane was barely controllable at such low airspeed and Michel knew that. It was a natural reflex action by the MIG pilot. Michel knew he would take evasive action and predicted the outcome exactly. The MIG was already at its low-speed performance limit, and as soon as the pilot applied the controls needed to take evasive action, it stalled abruptly, spinning into the ground.

I swear to God, as it rolled over, it missed the glider only by inches. I wet my pants when it happened. A normal reaction, I'm told, when you know for certain you're going to die. The MIG was too low to recover from a spin and exploded on impact with the ground. I suspect the pilot peed his pants too."

"My God!" Nicole gasped. "Michel never mentioned that."

Hollingsworth continued: "It shook us both up. Michel was prepared to die, right there, right that second. No doubt at all in my mind. After we both stopped shaking, I asked Michel what he would have done if the MIG hadn't taken evasive action. He said he would have rammed him, because we had nothing to lose. He was absolutely right, of course. The MIG would have shot the glider down unless we landed. We knew we would be captured if we landed and we both knew what the Muslims do to captured pilots. We weren't going to land! Your husband was a very smart and brave man. He saved us both from a horrible end that day."

"He always said that you risked your life for Israel to rescue him and couldn't quite understand why," replied Nicole, thoughtfully glancing over at Hollingsworth. Hollingsworth thought to himself, "it's a long story." but didn't elaborate.

Nicole picked him up at the hotel early the next day. The funeral was a befitting military event but without religious content, since Koudechah was not Jewish. Zabros made a short speech at the gravesite, praising Koudechah's exemplary military career and his key role in the preemptive attack on the UIA the previous year. The folded Israeli flag was presented to Madame Koudechah with all due ceremony, at which she cried. In honor of Michel she had abandoned her trademark red for black mourning-dress.

Simple, elegant and beautiful.

At the end of the ceremony, Gibli came over and welcomed Hollingsworth back to Israel. He invited him back to the Airforce Headquarters office, where Koudechah's staff had laid on a traditional "send-off", as Gibli put it. Turning to Nicole he said,

"Madame Koudechah will bring you in her car, I am sure."

Many of the people attending the send-off, including some of the young F35 pilots that Hollingsworth had trained, had worked on installing the early "homebuilt" IFF systems and were anxious to see Hollingsworth again to congratulate him on the success of the attack. Hollingsworth enjoyed the adulation of the young pilots, who knew about Koudechah's rescue in the glider. Several asked him if the story about downing the MIG was true. Hollingsworth assured them it was, and began to explain what had happened.

A crowd quickly gathered around him to hear the story. When he was finished there was no doubt, even in the minds of the skeptics, that they had downed a MIG with the glider. Hollingsworth declined to mention that he had wet his pants in the process.

Nicole came over to rescue him from the crowd, insisting that she was exhausted and needed to go home. She stopped at the hotel entrance and turned off the ignition.

"Can we have dinner together tomorrow?" Hollingsworth asked her in a tentative voice.

"I know you must be an emotional wreck, but I have to go back to the USA the day after tomorrow..." his voice trailed off.

"I need to be alone, Andrew," she replied with a forced smile. She retrieved a thick manila envelope from the glove compartment and handed it to him. "The scroll is in here, with the notes from Michel. It's very fragile, so try not to bend the envelope. Call me when you get back to the States." She kissed him softly on the cheek. "And get some sleep - you look tired."

"I promise!" Hollingsworth replied and got out of the car. As he turned to wave as he entered the hotel, she was already driving away.

Hollingsworth slept fitfully and woke up early, his internal clock still on San Francisco time. He made himself a cup of coffee and carefully opened the envelope that Nicole had given him. The one scroll that Koudechah had brought from the cave he had been hiding in before Hollingsworth found him, was sandwiched between two thick pieces of card and wrapped in a plastic cover. He unwrapped it carefully and saw that it was written in a script similar to the one he had seen on pictures of the Dead Sea Scrolls in a museum. He knew he would not be able to read it, so he carefully put it back between the pieces of card and replaced the plastic wrapping.

He started to go through Koudechah's notes. The first page was attached to a letter written in Hebrew; with a business letterhead he could not read. The note, in Koudechah's handwriting, simply said "Carbon dating of small section of Papyrus confirms same period as Dead Sea scrolls," followed by Koudechah's initials.

The next page had a yellow note in Koudechah's handwriting attached that said "Full translation by Rabbi David Cohen, Jerusalem." It was typed, double-spaced on plain paper. It appeared to be part of a description of a celebration that the prophet Mohamed had attended as young man, probably still a teenager. It described in lurid detail the debauchery that took place involving the young boys and adult men. It was unadulterated homosexual pornography. Hollingsworth was amazed and disgusted. He was no prude, but this was too much, and he moved on to read the other notes.

More than half of the remaining notes documented Koudechah's attempt to evade the missile, his ejection from the F16, and his trek from the crash site to the ridge of small hills where Hollingsworth had spotted him. It was a complete and detailed account of his survival in the desert. It would make a treatise for anyone wishing to study survival techniques. Koudechah had used every trick he knew to stay alive and cover nearly 25 kilometers per day toward the Turkish border, an amazing feat. The rest of the material was made up mostly of internet articles which described Mohamed's early life, where he had been, and the people with whom he had socialized. It was sparse and fragmented. Apparently not much was known about him until he began to represent himself as a messenger of Allah, the one and only God.

Hollingsworth got so engrossed in the narrative that Koudechah had left for him that he forgot about lunch. He lay down, intending to take a short nap, but woke up three hours later feeling hungry. He called for room service and ordered an "American Burger" and beer and settled down to do some more research on Mohamed's early life. He was surprised to learn that homosexuality had been prolific before the rise of Islam among certain tribes in what is now Saudi Arabia. He was beginning to understand why Koudechah thought that the scrolls might rock the Muslim faith. Homosexual behavior was still punishable by death in Saudi Arabia and some other Muslim nations.

He savored the last of the beer, packed all the materials back into the manila envelope, packed his travel bag, and went to bed early. Gibli was picking him up at six in the morning to take him to the airport. He fell asleep, disappointed that he had not had dinner with Nicole, and vowed that this time he would call her when he got home. He felt guilty that he had not been there for her in a time of great need.

Gibli arrived punctually, and they talked like old friends on the way to the airport. Gibli was anxious to tell Hollingsworth about developments in Israeli-Arab relations since, as Gibli put it, "they had whupped their Arab asses!" Apparently the UIA had begun to unravel. The old tribal conflicts re-emerged. Saudi-Arabia had lost the stability of the dictatorial Monarchy and begun to devolve into a theocracy worse than Iran. Trouble was brewing again and Gibli was trying to prepare Israel for more bitter skirmishes, but this time, with the individual Arab states who still surrounded them and still vowed to, someday, drive them into the sea.

Israeli-US relations, on the other had had flourished during Trump's second term, and Haley had vowed to support Israel as the only democracy in the Middle East. Haley vowed to "never allow the Arabs to get nuclear weapons, tactical or strategic." She backed this up with continued threats of "destroying" Iran's oil-dependent economy if they failed to conform to new anti-proliferation agreements. Quid pro quo had become the standard tool of US international relations.

Gibli dropped him at the airport, where Hollingsworth bought a Wall Street Journal and a car magazine with a photo of a

Porsche 911 on the front cover. In seven-and-a-half hours he would be home in Carmel. He wondered if has car was finished. He read the journal and looked at the car magazine pictures and watched two interminable movies, through which he dozed off several times.

The plane arrived in San Francisco at the very last gate on the longest concourse in the Airport, and Hollingsworth began the long trudge to Baggage Claim.

San Francisco

Peter picked Hollingsworth up at the airport. He had waited at the mobile phone park. He was driving Andrew's 911.

"Surprise," he yelled at Hollingsworth through the passenger window. "Your car was ready so I brought it. I was having my Cayenne serviced and they told me it was ready. I figured you would want to drive it back to Carmel." He laughed. "It's like a brand-new car. But it's not as nice as mine!" Peter had bought a new Porsche with his sign-on bonus.

As they drove back to the city, Peter filled Hollingsworth in on events at ERI.

"Things are crazy!" said Peter. "We've been buying up the old Nintendo Games as you know, but we are running out of parts. We've been reluctant to buy new parts from Japan because that will let our competition know what chips we're using in the systems. We scrub the markings off the old microprocessors and remark them with our numbers. It looks like we are going to have to start buying chips on the open market."

They talked about the new packaging and the huge order they just got to re-equip the Indian Airforce with IFF systems. Hollingsworth was having trouble absorbing the torrent of information when Peter said "We're going to the Paris Air Show this year. We have over 1000 installed units now, more than enough users to hold a product forum, and a load of new customers who want to see the product. I assume you'll be going."

Then without taking a breath, he asked, "Did you see Nicole in Tel Aviv."

"Yes, I did." Hollingsworth knew the question was coming and responded without offering any more news, which he knew Peter was dying to hear. They had arrived at the Porsche Specialist on Van Ness Avenue, and Peter pulled up next to his Cayenne.

Peter got out of the car and asked through the window, "So…?" Awaiting an answer on Nicole.

"Later!" Andrew responded, laughing, "I'll see you on Monday," and drove off, heading for Carmel.

He called Nicole as soon as he got home. Conversation was awkward at first and limited to accounts of their daily lives. At first, they talked mostly about work. But they began to call each other regularly, and gradually they opened up to each other again. She explained that she had felt guilty that he had lost his job because of the article about his speech at the Airshow. He countered that it had led to the dream job he had now. He confessed he hadn't called her because "the ball was in her court" and she had to decide what she was going to do about her marriage. She apologized for telling him right away that she was married and hadn't told him she had left Michel. Even though he had nearly killed her, she grieved at the death of her husband and didn't need Andrew in her life to do that.

She confided in Andrew that a German company had expressed some interest in buying the magazine and that, after Michel died, she had seriously considered it. Her heart wasn't in it anymore she, explained. It was time to do something else. She was going to meet the Germens at the Paris Airshow.

Andrew told her about the Public Offering and that his stock, which she had pointed out was only "paper", now had George

Washington's face printed on it. She was happy that it worked out and asked when he was going to buy one of those giant gliders. The laughed together a lot.

Life was better.

Paris

The plane arrived at Charles De Gaul International airport a few minutes early. ERI didn't have its own private jet like BA had. Hollingsworth missed that benefit of working for BA. As usual, he had shipped his baggage with the exhibit booth and carried only his small nylon parachute bag. While his fellow passengers went to get their baggage, he went directly to customs and immigration and was quickly processed. Rather than getting his usual Uber ride, he had decided to rent a car and drive himself to Le Bourget, where the Air Show was taking place.

Hollingsworth searched for the Hotel Renaissance on Google maps and soon found himself on Rue Chappelle. He soon regretted not taking the Route Peripherique, because the direct route via city streets was choked with traffic slowed down by hundreds of protestors. It took him over an hour to get to the hotel.

As usual, the lobby was packed with aviation industry people. Arabs, Chinese, Russians, Indians, Brits and a few Americans lined up four-deep at the registration desk. Hollingsworth quickly found George, the concierge, left his bag with him, and set off toward the Vendor registration desk, which was located on the third floor.

By the time Hollingsworth obtained his airshow credentials, it was late. He decided to get a quick bite to eat and get an early night. He wanted to take his favorite early morning walk.

He was up at 5:30 am and ate breakfast in the dining room. He was the only person there at that time in the morning. Afterward, he retraced the route he and Nicole had walked several times, two years ago. He strolled leisurely down the gravel pathway of the Terrace de Feullants, enjoying the statues and the architecture of the buildings along the Rue de Rivoli. As always, there was something satisfying about the crunch of the gravel underfoot. He saw the woman in red several hundred meters ahead, and knew immediately who it was. She was sitting on a park bench, waiting for him. Her mittens matched her French Blue beret. It could only be Nicole. He hadn't expected her.

She stood up as he approached and kissed him on both cheeks, affectionately this time.

"I sold the Magazine!" she exclaimed excitedly, and they began walking back toward the hotel. She stopped him before they left the walkway and turned to face him.

"Do you still love me?" she asked, looking up into his eyes.

"Yes, you know I do," he replied without hesitation.
"Good, then take me home with you after the show."

"To Carmel?" he asked

"Yes, to Carmel, California, USA"

"OK!" He smiled.

The End

Postscript

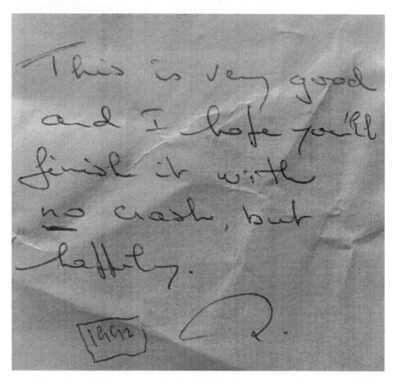

This is very good and I hope you'll finish it with no crash, but happily.

1992

Voila!

Made in the USA
Middletown, DE
31 January 2020